# MALTESE
# HEART

Isabelle Valente

Maltese Heart
Copyright © 2015 Isabelle Valente

Published by Love Leaf Publishing
www.loveleafpublishing.com

Cover and illustration
© 2015 Stephen Abela

ISBN: 978-1-911031-00-0

## DEDICATION

To my mother who has always supported me
and my spouse who continues to do so.
I love you both.

For my grandparents
and all those who continue to believe in love.

## PREFACE

As a teenager I dreamed of travelling and writing books.
This was my first foray into both. I wrote Maltese Heart in
the mid-1990s, when I was fifteen, at the time the world,
travel and airport security all seemed much simpler.

I did initially look at publishing the book but it all became
a little daunting for one so young (and naive). It wasn't until
some twenty years later that I decided to revisit it.

To that end I decided to release, this, my first novel. It
is what it is - the simple writings of a young person in love,
with both a place and a time.

Isabelle Valente

GOZO

Victoria

Mgarr

COMINO

Mellieha

MEDITERRANEAN
SEA

Mosta

Sliema
Valletta

Mdina

MALTA

Luqa
Airport

# CHAPTER ONE

The plane was stuffy with people a little too crowded together after a turbulent flight. Everyone's discomfort, prolonged by air traffic control over Malta, finally eased as the plane descended, its engines throbbing from the journey. All aboard sighed in relief as they felt the solid thud of the runway meeting the plane on landing. With the rapid decrease in speed the passenger's relief gave way to an eagerness to disembark. The fasten seat belt light was watched attentively, with a few rogues unbuckling ahead of time, in the hope it might mean they could breathe fresh air a little sooner.

A truck towing the steps came to the aeroplane quickly and the doors were popped open moments later. Daniel, his brother Phillip and friend Matthew were some of the first to leave. Climbing down the steps Phillip rubbed his ears and swung his rucksack onto his back, all at the same time, oblivious of the danger of knocking over those people behind him. It was only when Daniel pulled him towards the waiting bus that Phillip looked around to find a seat. Phillip sat down for the briefest of moments but Daniel pulled him back to his feet so that those more in need could be seated.

Once full the old bus lurched away making people and luggage bump against each other. Daniel thought it was a smooth ride compared to the local bone shakers – the buses that served as local transportation. He caught his reflection in the window; his eyes looked greener than usual contrasting with his dark brown hair and pale skin. All of the holidaymakers were rather pallid and he looked forward to feeling the morning heat of the sun on his skin. He knew that his family would comment on how pale they were. They always did. Their relatives would embrace them and welcome them back with a warmth that always made the boys glad to have returned.

Upon arriving at the check-in terminal the queues and paperwork began. There were those who were quite unprepared, fiddling with their passports and papers, desperately trying to find or borrow a pen. Others were well travelled and held themselves above such fumbling and gave the impression that somehow they shouldn't have to wait but they would endure it. Then there were the excited ones who were keen to see beyond the barren passport control booths and wanted to embrace new experiences and adventures. Daniel and his brother, Phillip, were already beginning to feel quite at home. They had been here many times before. It all looked the same as any other airport now; shining plastic, metal and glass but before it was a small place oozing character. Those were different times and now nothing but childhood memories.

Once through immigration, the process continued with collecting luggage before wheeling a deranged baggage cart through customs and out into the arrivals lounge. There they found their travel representative, who seemed to meet all the pre-requisites, overly tanned, fixed smile, a gaudy company uniform and clip board with a checklist of names. She ticked their names and directed them to the coach.

The coach had an abundance of space with very few people on board as it weaved from Luqa airport towards Sliema. In the distant night sky were the lights of small towns. Daniel's mind drifted to a memory from years ago when his father had brought them to the island and hired a car. His father had asked what car they should get and he had said a yellow car. That was the only provision he had made as a child: the colour. The car was yellow but that was about the only satisfactory thing about it. There was no such thing as air conditioning, save for trying to wind the jammed windows down. The seat belts didn't move, the transmission was shot and it broke down on several occasions leaving them somewhere in the middle of nowhere. Despite it all those were happier times and the reason why Malta had become like home to them. The palm trees cast a strange shape in the night sky compared to England's more traditional deciduous trees but it was all familiar and comforting. As the coach entered Sliema Daniel gazed at the yachts; docked in the harbour forming a silhouette against the dark sky. Beams of moonlight shimmered off their polished surfaces and was captured in the gentle rippling of the waves.

On the other side of the road was a long row of

shops and hotels. The buildings were all white and cream coloured to help keep them cool. Only the church really stood out from the rest. Hewn from limestone with tall dominating spires and beautiful stained glass windows. The doors were solid wood with large metal hinges making the place seem impenetrable but the illuminated façade counteracted the fortifications to make it appear welcoming. After the church it was more of the same white buildings, some with side streets running alongside them, others crammed in between larger buildings without the slightest gap. A few moments later the coach stopped and they stepped out. As they waited for the luggage to be taken out of the storage hold Daniel felt the breeze coming from the sea. It was refreshing compared to the recirculated air of the plane and stagnant air inside the coach. He watched and waited for the last suitcase, his brother's, to be removed and then the three of them entered the hotel where they joined the end of the queue at reception.

The reception was part of the lobby area, a large sweeping open space with comfortable chairs along one wall and a small shop next to the reception. The ground floor went off to either side of the reception to the lifts and the stairs. The receptionist made quick work of checking people in, taking their names, checking home addresses, disseminating relevant information as needed or requested and then handing out the keys. Daniel stepped forward and said,

"Daniel and-"

"Welcome back," said the receptionist with a surprisingly genuine tone considering the late hour and repetitive nature of his job.

Daniel, Phillip and Matthew didn't quite know what

to say beyond,

"Thank you."

"Your uncle stopped by earlier," said the receptionist answering their unasked question and handing them their key. "You are on the top floor – the suite. Take the express elevator on the left."

"Thank you," said Daniel taking the key and passing it to Phillip.

Tired from the journey they went to their room at the far end of the hotel. As they entered the room Phillip struggled to find the slot where the key card had to be inserted. He fumbled in the dark until he finally slotted the card in place and all the lights came on. They had been expecting a single room with an extra cot but they found themselves in a suite of three rooms. The first room, which they were standing in, was a lounge, complete with mini bar, writing desk and television. The next two rooms were the bedrooms along with the bathrooms. They looked at each other searching for an explanation.

"Quite the upgrade," said Phillip.

Daniel saw a card on the table, along with a welcome basket containing snacks and drinks.

"Courtesy of Uncle Rocco," read Daniel.

"It is good to have family," said Phillip.

Matthew opened the door to the balcony and they all stepped out and looked over the harbour. Across the bay was Valletta, the capital. No matter how many times they saw that view it always impressed them. Behind the safety of the massive fortified walls a whole city of people slept, waiting for the coming dawn, as they had done for generations. After the long trip they got settled into their rooms and hoped to get a good night's rest.

The following morning Daniel woke before the

others. He quietly got dressed and ready to go down for breakfast in the hotel restaurant. He passed through the interconnecting bedroom and then through the lounge so that he could leave their rooms. The door closer almost slammed the door shut but he managed to stop it just in time with his foot and then closed it softly. Daniel walked down the long white corridor looking at the prints of local art work. Most were pictures of native flowers but some were prints of people. Arriving at the lift he pushed the button, waited and then stepped into it. The lift was small, just large enough for four people perhaps five or six at a squash but certainly not the stated number of eight. The lift stopped on the ground floor where Daniel walked out and headed past the reception area and across to the other side, where there was a small corridor leading to another lift that only went up and down one floor. Walking past the lift Daniel used the spiralling staircase which coiled round a central point, where a water feature had been created with a dark looking rock that water trickled down into a small pool. Once at the bottom of the stairs he could see that the restaurant was busy. So Daniel decided to have a quick look around. On the lower level along with the restaurant was a separate bar, a gym, an indoor swimming pool, an outdoor pool and sunbathing area overlooking the bay. He returned to the restaurant and entered through the glass doors and saw the self-service buffet breakfast. Daniel took some cereals and a glass of milk and then made his way to an empty table. He had finished his bowl of cereal when Matthew and Phillip arrived. They fetched their own breakfasts and joined him. Phillip's hearing had not fully returned after the flight and so he compensated for it by speaking louder and louder.

"Morning little brother," said Phillip.

Daniel mouthed the word, "Morning," back to Phillip knowing he would not hear him and looked at Matthew.

"You look tired," said Daniel.

"Someone was snoring."

Phillip did not hear or perhaps he chose not to.

"You were snoring again," Daniel said as loud as he dared to Phillip.

"I do not snore," said Phillip.

Matthew shook his head,

"If he does it again then we're swapping rooms."

Daniel chuckled.

"Any plans for our first day?" asked Matthew.

"I thought we could make the walk into Valletta, so we could meet with our grandparents. They said they were looking forward to seeing you again so you have to come too."

"I'd like to see them again."

"Of course I'm not sure if Phillip is up for the walk."

"What?" said Phillip recognising the sound of his own name.

"We're walking to Valletta," said Matthew loudly.

"Every time," said Phillip to Daniel, "you insist on walking five miles there and back."

"It's a tradition," said Daniel.

Daniel could see that Phillip wasn't interested. He knew his brother well enough to know that he would much prefer to sit on a beach and read a book the whole time.

"How about we catch the bus on the return leg?" asked Daniel.

"Fine," agreed Phillip.

After breakfast they returned to the room where

Phillip flung his tattered book into his bag and then sat down in front of the television waiting impatiently for Matthew and Daniel even though they only took a few moments more to get ready. They left the hotel and headed into the main centre of Sliema where the tourist shops sold the same postcards, leather goods and anything with the Maltese cross as they had for several decades. After following the coast line for a while they reached the bridge to Manoel Island. They had no reason to cross over as it would only extend their journey but it was an escape from the hustle and bustle of the shops and holiday makers. They were very much on their own as they crossed over and began walking past the sailing boats and mostly abandoned buildings. They continued beyond the first rows of buildings to the ruins of an old fort, which provided them with a better view of Valletta. The massive fortified walls of the capital showed the signs of their age and use over the centuries from damage by cannon fire to the bullet wounds of the Second World War. Behind the walls the cream coloured buildings towering upwards with the large dome of the church prominent against the sky line. Despite it all being a man-made structure it seemed almost natural, as if it had been formed there like stalagmites in a cave, as if the sky had slowly deposited the city over thousands of years. At that moment Daniel thought it would have been the perfect place to stop and do nothing, something his brother would enjoy. However it was Phillip who wanted to move on and so they returned to the mainland where they stopped at a small café and sat outside with a glass bottle of soda and passively observed the hustle and bustle of the tourists and the locals. It was at the café that Phillip took advantage of the break and started to read his book but Daniel and Matthew stopped him before he became too engrossed so that they could continue on their way.

They continued following the coastal path around through Gzira, Ta' Xbiex, Msida, Pieta, Floriana and into Valletta. There they spent some time looking around the market in Castille Place, where there was a tremendous variety of products ranging from clothes to music. The more interesting things were on some of the local craft stalls. One stall which caught their eye was selling hand crafted wooden plates which created a three dimensional image of a famous Maltese landscape. Daniel appreciated their beauty and the skill taken to make them especially when compared to the mass produced tourist souvenirs they had seen earlier that morning. From the market Phillip led the way to their grandparents flat. It was in the heart of the city and their flat was on the top floor. Daniel was ready to race Phillip to the top as they had done since they were children but his brother shook his head and plodded up the stairs. That didn't stop Daniel from dashing ahead. By the time Matthew and Phillip had caught up with him their grandfather, William, was at the door. William's light grey hair surrounded the side of his head and his glasses were getting thicker and thicker as his eyesight was not as good as it used to be but his mind was sharp and he recognised them all at once,

"Daniel, Phillip, come in, come in. Ah Matthew you came back. Come in my boy, come in."

William was ushering them into the dining room, past the kitchen from which their grandmother, Violet, emerged. She was wearing her apron and had already started making tea for them all. Her hair was dyed a reddish-brown colour and she too had thick, dark tinted glasses. Violet did not move as well as she used to. She was a lot shorter than the boys and seemed to be shrinking. None of that stopped her from greeting them all with a welcoming hug and kiss on each cheek,

"Boys, it has been too long. You look so pale. You need some sun. Come in, come in."

They followed William and Violet into the dining room where they sat around the large family dining table.

"The tea Vi," said William.

Violet raised her hands and head and made a little noise in vexation before she went back out to fetch the tea whilst William began the small talk,

"How was the flight?"

"A little bumpy but okay," answered Daniel.

"And the hotel?"

"It's nice," the three of them answered.

"Ah good. I stopped and talked to the manager last week. Did you know I went to school with his father?"

They all shook their heads but it wasn't really a surprise. It was a small island and William was well known to a great many people.

"Vi, how's that tea coming?" William called to his wife.

"I'll go and help," said Daniel getting up.

He went to the kitchen, where his grandmother had the tea ready but was finding it difficult to carry the tray with the heavy tea pot, cups, saucers and selection of biscuits. Daniel took the tray for her and walked slowly with Violet back to the dining room, where she began to serve the tea.

"It is good to see you all," said Violet. "It has been too long."

"Two years," replied Phillip.

"Too long," added Daniel.

"You are all well?" asked Violet.

They all nodded and said,

"Yes."

"And your mother?"

"She's well," said Daniel.

"And your family Matthew?"

"They are okay."

"That's good."

"You had a good flight?" asked Violet.

They said yes and gave her the recap of the flight and hotel story thus far. The pleasantries continued with updates from home, the people they all knew and cared about, the weather and how their grandparents missed visiting England for the cold and rain because the heat was too much that year. William was excited to tell them about the changes in Malta whilst Violet wanted to know about their personal lives. She was worried that they were all getting too old not to be in serious relationships. They each gave their own pre-defined set of answers on the subject that they had been giving for years. As Daniel found himself running through his own rhetoric it sounded hollower than ever. He wondered if there really was something missing in his life especially as he looked at his grandparents, who had been married for over fifty years. Could there be someone out there with whom he wanted to spend the rest of his life with? He did not know and he had spent a little too much time convincing himself that he was accustomed to the idea of spending his life alone.

By the time they left they had drank far too much tea which made the bone shaker of a bus ride back to the hotel more than a little uncomfortable. After a little time for adjustment they were content to settle down for the evening in the hotel bar. The bar was in one corner with seats and tables over the rest of the area. Matthew ordered them drinks and brought them over to their table. Daniel looked round at the room. It had a dark brown brick interior with a few large local artists' prints on the walls. Around the centrally located dance floor were several support pillars for the building, wrapped with wooden trellises over which some kind of climbing plants grew. Scattered around the bar there were groups, families, elderly couples, a few younger couples and the occasional loners who might have been waiting for someone or simply enjoying time by themselves. Daniel continued looking at all the people, only partially listening to their own conversation about the day and what plans they had. He noticed a group of three girls. Matthew was quick to catch on to his lingering gaze,

"Looks like someone has your attention?"

Daniel wasn't used to having anyone more attentive than his brother and looked back at Matthew,

"Sorry. I was elsewhere."

"I could tell," said Matthew.

Only then did Phillip begin to look around trying to figure out what had been of interest to his brother and Matthew. At first he did not notice anything particularly interesting, until he too saw the three girls.

"Hey, look at those girls," said Phillip as if he no one else had noticed. "Over there."

Phillip motioned like a seal bobbing its head.

"Subtle. Really subtle," said Daniel.

Phillip shrugged. Subtlety was not in his nature and he made that clear by continuing to stare at the three girls even whilst he continued drinking.

"Maybe you should introduce yourself?" said Daniel.

Phillip's eyes seemed transfixed on one of the girls, she had long dark hair and a beauty spot on her left cheek but his brother's suggestion broke his stare and he finally looked back at his friends.

"I don't know," said Phillip.

Matthew was keeping quiet. Daniel looked back at the girls. For a moment he felt his heart race. It beat all the quicker as one of the girls got up and walked towards them. She was tall with light brown, shoulder length hair which curled at the bottom. Her lips were pale red but seemed vivid in comparison to her complexion and her eyes sparkled. Daniel wondered if she had heard their discussion, or worse found their long lingering looks unwanted. He looked down at the table and his drink as she came closer and closer. At that moment he had never felt more a coward. All he would be capable of was fumbling over a few words and making himself seem like an idiot. She was so close to them now he could sense her presence. His brother was tracking her too but he wasn't afraid to look or to stare. Phillip watched her walk out of the bar,

"You're safe little brother. She's gone."

Daniel was almost afraid to glance behind him but he had to see for himself that she had left. The other two women had also stood up but they had gone to the bar. Phillip straightened himself up,

"Well I think it is time to make some introductions. Right Matthew?"

Matthew felt nearly as much panic as Daniel but neither of them could stop Phillip. He had already stood up, crossed over to them, and was introducing himself,

"Ladies."

The girl with dark hair smiled at him, the other girl

with lighter blonde hair was not quite as welcoming but it did not deter Phillip. Most men might lack the confidence to continue but Daniel knew his brother too well. He could play cards with the devil and win. It took less than two minutes for him to break the ice, make them laugh and invite them back to their table. Phillip made the introductions as if he had known the girls as long as he had his own brother and best friend,

"Sarah and Lisa, this is my brother Daniel, and good friend Matthew."

They all exchanged awkward half-standing handshakes before sitting down together. Phillip ensured he sat next to Lisa, the girl with dark hair. It amazed Daniel and Matthew how quickly he seemed to have her at ease, so much so that with the excuse of fetching another drink the two of them relocated to the bar. The remaining three stumbled for any kind of conversation but remained sat together for what would be considered a polite amount of time before Sarah excused herself,

"Thank you for the drink. I have to check on our friend."

"Good night," said Daniel and Matthew.

Daniel wondered if he could find a way to ask Sarah about her friend but she was leaving. As she left she looked at Lisa and Phillip but they did not notice her and appeared inseparable. Sarah turned round and walked back to Matthew,

"Could you tell them that I've gone up?"

"Yes," said Matthew.

"Maybe we can see you all tomorrow?" asked Daniel

It was a feeble attempt but all he could manage. Sarah did not seem certain but she looked back at her friend and then at Matthew once more,

"Maybe."

With that Sarah departed glancing back at Matthew. Daniel saw Matthew's look of surprise and shouldered him gently. Matthew shrugged his response. The communication was minimal but more than sufficient for them. They both finished their drinks and headed out of the hotel to walk along the sea front. The temperature was perfect, the atmosphere vibrant with the salt water hanging in the air and the sound of the waves lapping at the shore.

"It looks like things have changed," said Daniel looking around.

"More so here than in Valletta," said Matthew.

"I wonder how much trouble Phillip is going to cause this time."

"There's always something."

"Yes there is."

"Although maybe this time he won't be the only one?"

"I don't know what you mean," said Daniel.

"We'll see," replied Matthew.

"It's good to be away," said Daniel changing the subject.

"Yes. No work for two whole weeks."

"Although that is two weeks with Phillip."

"That's a different kind of work."

"That it is," said Daniel

"It will be fine. We can take our time. See some new places, well new for me," said Matthew.

"There's still places I haven't seen and those I'd like to visit again."

"So we are good to go and if we have to bail Phillip out of trouble a few times then that's what we do."

"It doesn't feel quite the same this time."

"What doesn't?"

"Being back here."

"It's only been a day."

"I know. Things are familiar but it feels like there is something missing."

"It's probably just because things have changed. Things are changing."

"I guess so."

"It can be hard to make the transition from education to work or any stage of life. I'm sure that's all it is."

"Sometimes I wonder if Phillip feels the same way."

"I couldn't say. Everything moves so quickly these days. All you can do is try and keep moving along as best you can."

Daniel and Matthew continued talking and walking for a little while. He tried to think over what they said. About how his life was in a state of flux but he did not feel that that was the problem. It felt as if there were a part of him that was missing and he had hoped that returning to Malta would somehow help fill that void.

When they returned to the hotel they went straight to the bar to see if Phillip was still there. He wasn't and so they went to the room. Neither of them had the key so they had to knock on the door and wait. There was no answer. A little look of frustration passed between Daniel and Matthew and so they knocked again a bit louder, and again, and again until Phillip cracked open the door a couple of inches. He was topless and a bit out of breath and looked uncomfortable. Daniel tried to push the door open further but Phillip put his weight behind it to stop him.

"Can we come in?" asked Matthew.

Daniel looked past Phillip and saw a trail of clothes

leading to the first bedroom where he saw a girl's leg, Lisa's he presumed, dangling over the edge of the bed. He glanced at Phillip who turned and tried to kick a few of the clothes into the bedroom before closing the door. Returning to the main door, Phillip opened it and let Daniel and Matthew in.

"Um," muttered Phillip.

"Can we go through?" asked Matthew.

Phillip shook his head and looked at them sheepishly. Daniel looked at the couch and turned back to his brother.

"Shall we sleep on the couch then?" asked Daniel.

"That would be great," said Phillip without a hint of hesitation as he sped back into the bedroom.

Neither Daniel nor Matthew had a chance to express any further objections as the bedroom door firmly closed and they heard a series of giggles that they hoped were from Lisa and not Phillip. They both knew it was going to be an uncomfortable night. Matthew turned to Daniel,

"Couch or floor?"

## Chapter Two

As Jenny was leaving the bar she walked past one of the young men who had been glancing over at her and her friends, Sarah and Lisa. She was tempted to stop, to say something but she was afraid. He looked handsome. Perhaps a little shy as he was nervously still and looking down at the table. She wanted him to look at her again but she did not know what she would do if he did. Perhaps if she was as forthright as Lisa she could stop right there and demand his attention but she did not feel able to do anything so bold. Jenny continued out of the bar and up to her room. Her room consisted of a lounge from which a door led to the bedroom. The lounge was furnished much the same as Daniel's suite, the same white wallpaper, grey carpet, settee but only one comfortable chair. Jenny went through to the bedroom, kicked off her shoes, and dropped down on the bed. She lay there for several minutes getting frustrated with herself,

"Come on," she said to herself, "you can do better than this."

She sat up and moved to the edge of the bed thinking about putting her shoes back on and re-joining her friends at the bar. Her shoes were black, high heeled, and went with anything but they really hurt her feet. They were calling to her, telling her to put them back on. They promised that this time things would be different, they wouldn't hurt so much. She knew they lied.

There was a knock on the door. It was Sarah,

"How are you doing?"

"Sorry, I was a little tired," said Jenny.

"That's okay. I'm calling it a night myself."

Jenny was glad she wasn't the only one.

"What about Lisa?" asked Jenny.

"I think we'll both have a room to ourselves tonight."

"That didn't take long."

"It never does."

"What about you?" asked Sarah.

"What about me?"

"I saw you looking."

"I couldn't," said Jenny blushing.

"Why not?" asked Sarah. "He's tall, dark and handsome. What more do you need?"

Jenny thought for a moment. The memory of him burned in her mind but there were so many questions. What if he wasn't nice? What if he was some kind of creep? Her heart sank a little as she thought about it. The one guy already hooked up with Lisa. What if he was the same? Wouldn't she be the same if she did have a fling with him? What if he already had a girlfriend, a fiancée, a wife or all of the above?

"That's not why I came on holiday," said Jenny.

"I know but it wouldn't hurt. I mean..."

"I couldn't. It isn't fair."

"It doesn't have to be fair. It only has to be fun."

"Perhaps," said Jenny looking lost.

"Hey, it's okay. I was only teasing."

Sarah hugged Jenny and said,

"It doesn't matter. I only want you to be happy."

"I am and I'm glad we're all here together."

"That's what friends are for."

Sarah began to leave, as she was at the exit she asked,

"What do you feel like doing tomorrow?"

Jenny did not want to tell her, she knew her friends did not share her passion for architecture especially Lisa. It seemed that Sarah read her mind,

"Don't worry I don't think Lisa will be with us tomorrow. So it's your choice."

"Well I read about a church in a place called Mosta. It is supposed to have the third largest unsupported dome in Europe."

"Oh I can hardly wait," said Sarah flippantly as she pulled off her high heeled shoes. "I won't be wearing these tomorrow."

"Thank you," said Jenny.

"Anything for you; even going to Church on a weekday."

As Sarah left she wished Jenny goodnight and told her to get some rest and that they would go down together for breakfast.

The next morning Jenny and Sarah took a twenty minute taxi ride over to Mosta. The driver took them right up to the front steps of the St. Marija Assunta Church or as he called it Mosta Dome. From the outside the church was ornate, made from the same local stone that had been quarried on the island for centuries. Its columns linked two bell towers on each side and provided only a deceptive view of the dome behind them. Jenny was fascinated as she tried to absorb every detail as they made their way inside. The interior took her breath away. The rotunda was a visual feast with archways, paintings, murals, decorations and altars. As her eyes tracked upwards she saw the upper ring with windows all around letting the light pour in. Above that was the dome itself. It spanned more than thirty metres across and was completely unsupported. No columns, joists or beams. A pure dome as lovingly crafted as the rest of the church with a swirling pattern of diamonds flowing up to the peak. Jenny was still looking around when Sarah called her attention to something that appeared very out of place.

"Is that a bomb?" asked Sarah.

They both went over to it and looked at the bomb and then read the surrounding plaques that told the story. On the ninth of April, 1942 during the Second World War a two hundred kilogram bomb came crashing through the roof of the dome and fell amongst the congregation of over three hundred people. It never exploded. The bomb had its detonator removed and later the replica was placed in the church. Jenny felt goose bumps and a shiver run through her.

"Could you imagine?"

"No."

Jenny looked from the bomb to where the photograph had shown the hole in the ceiling and shook her head in disbelief. Other pictures showed the people at the time and the real bomb. They looked back at the bomb on display and read the words over again, 'il-miraklu tal-bomba'. The part that transfixed Jenny was the word miracle. As they began to leave the church the thought of the miracle bomb remained with them and Jenny asked Sarah,

"Do you think there really are any miracles?"

"I don't know."

It was an impossible question for either of them to answer. It seemed strange that if miracles did exist they were reduced to tourist attractions.

"I haven't practised my faith in a long time but perhaps we should light a candle," said Sarah.

Jenny was not sure so Sarah continued,

"To remember the past and perhaps hope that miracles still exist."

Jenny could not fault her logic. It was good that people should remember and there was no shortage of people in need of miracles. They both made a small contribution and lit two candles. Whilst Sarah defaulted to the indoctrination of her youth and knelt in silent prayer Jenny stood by her side feeling alone with her own thoughts. Her loneliness was quickly dissipated as Sarah, still kneeling took her hand and held it tightly. In that moment their experience became a shared one and one that neither of them would ever talk about again.

Upon returning to Sliema the two friends lost track of time in the main shopping district. They indulged in a little retail therapy in an attempt to mask any deeper thoughts that had been stirred by their experience earlier in the day. Only as the sun was setting did they find their way back to the hotel and then the bar. On entering the bar Sarah saw Daniel and Matthew. Jenny was hesitant to join them but Sarah took her arm and piloted her along. It was clear Matthew was glad to see Sarah but she did not know how Daniel felt. She hoped he did not feel as out of place as she did. Sarah managed the introductions,

"Jenny, Daniel. Daniel, Jenny."

She smiled at him but had no idea what to say. Conversation was not her speciality and the gaps and silent pauses indicated that it was not his either. The trivial small talk resulted in the most basic of responses. None of which solicited in-depth conversation. Jenny missed Lisa, it was too quiet without her. Sarah and Matthew were trying to keep things going but it was all rather difficult. Jenny wished Daniel would look at her like he had the night before but he could hardly raise his eye-line.

"This is kind of awkward isn't it?" asked Jenny with the briefest flash of a smile.

Her smile caught his attention and Daniel lifted his head a little higher. She smiled again and he began to look at her properly.

"I've never been great with small talk, that's my brother's thing."

Jenny looked over at Matthew but did not see much of a family resemblance.

"Matthew is a friend. My brother is…"

"With Lisa."

"Yeah. Sorry about that."

Jenny laughed,

"Why are you sorry?"

"I don't know because sometimes Phillip makes things kind of awkward."

Jenny was amused and intrigued,

"He keeps you busy?"

There was no chance for Daniel to answer as Lisa came into the bar, staggering and obviously tipsy. She went over to her friends.

"Aww look at all of you," she said fondling Jenny's hair. "You're so pretty."

"Okay," said Jenny looking at Daniel who saw she had her own Phillip to contend with, which raised a good question.

"Where's Phillip?" asked Daniel.

"Oh Jen, I'm so glad you're here," said Lisa.

"That's nice but where's Phillip?" asked Jenny.

"He's going for a swim."

Daniel looked over at Matthew and they knew this was nothing but trouble. They stood up quickly and ran towards the hotel's swimming pool.

"Hey, where're they going?" asked Lisa.

"The swimming pool," said Sarah.

"Why?"

"To find Phillip," said Jenny.

"We're going swimming," said Lisa getting up and leaving.

Jenny and Sarah caught up with her.

"Why don't we get you to bed?" said Sarah.

Lisa was not listening and staggered forwards and rounded the corner that led to the pool. Jenny and Sarah kept following when they heard a squelching sound. They went round the corner and saw Phillip standing there fully dressed and soaking wet. He was leaning on Daniel who, for his trouble, was also getting drenched. Phillip pulled off his wet shoes and gave them to Matthew who did not really want them. Lisa approached Phillip,

"Aww you went swimming without me."

"I'm sorry. We can go back," said Phillip.

Lisa handed her purse and shoes to Matthew and started towards the pool forcing Jenny to stop her.

Phillip turned to go back as well but Daniel pulled him away. Together they began trying to coax the pair back towards the lift in the hope they might get them back to their rooms. As they approached Phillip looked at the restaurant.

"I'm gonna go eat," said Phillip.

"No you're not," said Daniel. "You're soaking wet."

"You're right my liddle broder."

Jenny saw the flash of irritation on Daniel's face. He was much taller than his brother and clearly did not like the supposed term of endearment. They thought they had the situation under control until Phillip started to strip. He pulled off his shirt revealing the slight gut from too much drinking and would have dropped his trousers had Daniel not stopped him.

"What are you doing?" asked Daniel.

"I'm getting changed."

"Let's do that in the room, okay?" said Daniel pulling Phillip into the elevator.

Matthew picked up the wet shirt to go with the still dripping shoes. The lift went up one floor to the lobby. All they had to do next was cross the reception desk and get to the main lifts. Jenny peeked out from the corridor and saw that there was a night porter at the desk. She winced, uncomfortable with the thought of making a scene. Matthew had a similar thought and tried to persuade Phillip to put his shirt back on but was having no success. Phillip's attention had returned to Lisa and they were starting to get a little too friendly in public. Once more Daniel had to pull his brother away. He looked at Jenny,

"I really am sorry."

Jenny smiled at him and he marched Phillip along as

if nothing was wrong. The others fell in line and walked past swiftly. The night porter raised his eyebrow when he saw Phillip, half naked and soaking wet. Then he saw Jenny and Sarah all but carrying Lisa. He made a little ahem sound to which Daniel replied,

"Good evening."

"Evening," added Matthew.

Jenny tried not to look at the porter but she could feel him staring and so said,

"Evening," and as they were almost past, "sorry."

The night porter gave a little shrug and paid them no more attention. Phillip continued trying to go in any other direction than the one he should which forced Daniel to strong arm him all the way into the main lift. They got them both inside and Matthew asked,

"Which floor?"

"Five," said Sarah.

Matthew pushed the buttons and the doors closed. They all stood there waiting as the lift's cables and pulleys whirred into motion. The chime sounded and the doors opened to the fifth floor. Matthew and Sarah stepped out first and turned to wait for the others. Jenny was having a difficult time trying to drag Lisa away from Phillip, despite Daniel standing in between them, so Sarah handed her purse to Matthew and helped to separate them. Together Jenny and Sarah got Lisa out of the lift and headed towards their room. Matthew followed them and Daniel was not far behind with Phillip. At the room Jenny and Sarah got their friend into her bed as gently as possible. The boys arrived and on seeing the empty bed Phillip collapsed into it. Daniel tried to pull him up,

"You need to get to your own bed."

"No. I'm sleepy," said Phillip.

"Why don't you leave him here?" said Jenny. "Sarah can sleep with me tonight."

Daniel and Matthew looked at each other and then back at Phillip who already looked half asleep and agreed. Jenny and Sarah tucked Lisa up whilst Daniel attempted to remove the worst of Phillip's wet clothes before throwing a blanket over him. They left the room and walked down the corridor.

"They are quite the pair," said Sarah.

"Two peas in a pod," said Jenny.

"Two people who are going to be very hung over tomorrow," said Matthew.

They stopped several doors down outside Jenny's room.

"This is us," said Jenny opening the door.

They all lingered outside for a few moments. Seeing Daniel soaking wet Jenny put her hand on his chest and said,

"You should get out of those wet clothes too."

She felt his heart beat and they both blushed even though her meaning was clear. Sarah bid Matthew goodnight and went inside the room whilst he went towards the lifts. Both left swiftly as if they had intruded on a private moment. Jenny's hand was still on Daniel's chest, his heart was beating faster now, and he was looking directly in her eyes. She blinked and pulled her hand away.

"Well, goodnight," she said and slowly moved inside and closed the door.

"Goodnight," said Daniel as the door was all but closed.

Inside the room Sarah was looking at Jenny,

"What was that?"

"Nothing… I don't know."

It was a lie. A very clear and obvious lie and neither of them believed it.

## CHAPTER THREE

Daniel headed towards the elevators but Matthew was gone. He looked back at Jenny's room. He could still feel her touch. It seemed to have filled his chest with warmth and he wanted nothing more than to go back and see her again but he didn't know how he could. As he waited for the lift he kept looking back at her room and it was only reluctantly he left it behind. On returning to his room he knocked and Matthew let him in.

"What was that?" asked Matthew.

"I don't know," said Daniel dropping down onto the nearest seat.

There was no explanation other than he wanted to see her and feel her touch again. He could not think of anything else. It took him a while to realise Matthew was looking at him. Had he said something? Daniel did not know, it took a moment for his mind to come back into focus. Matthew was talking,

"I forgot them."

"Forgot what? Sorry?"

"The purses and shoes."

Daniel looked over to the table where they were.

"Don't worry I'll take them back."

He wanted to see Jenny again and so he took the items and walked back through the corridor, into the lift, and to Jenny's door. At that moment he stopped, he was nervous and questioned what he was doing. His logical mind told him it was simple. All he was doing was bringing her friend's purse back. That was a convincing enough argument for him and so Daniel knocked on the door. It was the only choice he could have made. There was no response and so he knocked again and then he heard footsteps. For a second he panicked. What would Jenny think? Did she like him? What kind of a thought was that? What happened in that moment when she touched him? The door opened and Jenny stood there in her nightgown. It was white with a flower pattern in parts that made it semi-transparent. The gown had a low cut front and Daniel completely forgot what he was doing there.

Jenny looked at him and saw the purses and shoes and invited him inside,

"Come in."

The back of her gown was cut down almost to the bottom of her spine. Daniel tried not to look at her but he couldn't help it.

"Come in," she said again softly.

Daniel didn't realise he hadn't moved until that moment and so stepped inside.

"I just got out of the shower."

He could still hear the shower running.

"Sarah's in there now."

"Oh. I…"

"Thank you," said Jenny taking the things from Daniel. Her hands brushed against his and just like when she placed her hand on his chest he lost track of time. He watched her set the purses and shoes down and he wondered how his heart was pounding so much? What was he doing there? He did not know.

"I thought I'd better bring them back," said Daniel.

"Yes, thank you," repeated Jenny.

"I should go," he said not moving.

Jenny smiled at him.

"Unless you want a quick nightcap?"

Daniel nodded and said,

"No more alcohol though."

She laughed and he wanted to hear her laugh again.

"Hot chocolate?" she asked him.

He nodded again.

"Sit down," she said gently.

Daniel obeyed and felt his wits slowly returning until she turned and walked towards the kettle. The curve of her back was tantalising. The ridges of her spine moved ever so slightly with every step she took. There was steam already rising from the spout. Daniel watched her as she took a second cup and put the powder in before pouring out the water. As she brought Daniel his cup he could smell the delicate fragrance of her skin. He was completely mesmerised and watched as she sat down and carefully pulled her legs up onto the seat resting her knees on the arm of the chair. She gazed at him and said,

"Quite a night."

"That's Phillip."

"And Lisa."

"They'll be rough tomorrow."

"Yes they will."

Daniel sipped the hot chocolate, it burned a little. His mind was racing with so many thoughts. This wasn't normal for him. He wasn't the one who found himself in such situations. He left that kind of thing to his brother.

"They make quite a pair," said Jenny.

"I hope that we haven't ruined your plans?"

"We didn't really have any."

"Maybe I could help make it up to you?"

"You don't have anything to make up for."

"No, I know, but he's my brother and, well, I've been cleaning up after him for a long time."

"But isn't he your big brother?"

"Yes but our roles are kind of reversed."

Daniel realised that the shower had stopped and he heard Sarah in the bedroom.

"I should probably get going," Daniel said setting down his drink, "maybe we could meet for breakfast?"

"That would be nice."

With that Daniel started towards the door. Jenny got up and came over to see him out. He wanted to kiss her goodbye, but was worried it would be inappropriate. They both paused at the doorway. Neither certain of how to say good night. There was no kiss, or embrace. They were startled by Sarah opening the bedroom door. Like guilty teenagers Daniel quickly left and Jenny closed the door behind him pretending no one had ever been there despite the evidence to the contrary.

The next morning Daniel woke up as he heard footsteps close to him. He opened his eyes and saw

Matthew.

"Good morning," said Matthew.

"Morning," replied Daniel getting up and feeling like he hadn't slept at all.

"How do you think the patients are this morning?"

"Pretty awful if there's any justice."

They both got ready and were heading down towards the hotel restaurant for breakfast, when they stepped into the lift Daniel told Matthew,

"I asked Jenny for breakfast."

Matthew did not say anything but pressed the fifth floor button. The lift descended and they got out and went over to Jenny's door where Daniel knocked. Sarah answered,

"Hi. We're nearly ready."

They waited for a minute and then Jenny joined them and asked,

"Do you think we should check on them?"

"I think we should," said Daniel.

They went along the corridor and quietly opened Sarah and Lisa's room. It was dark but they could just make out Lisa moving and they could hear Phillip snoring.

"Well they're fine," said Matthew.

They closed the door behind them and continued down to the lobby where Daniel saw a familiar face.

"Uncle Rocco."

"Daniel. You get taller every time I see you. Where's your brother? Still in bed?"

"Yeah. I think he'll be there most of the morning."

"Nothing too serious?"

"Not at all."

"So it's Matthew and…" said Rocco seeing Jenny and Sarah, "your friends?"

Daniel could not answer for them. The two girls looked at each other uncertainly but Rocco walked straight over to them and putting himself in the middle began to lead them out of the hotel.

"So, I take us all out for breakfast," said Rocco.

"Oh we couldn't," said Jenny. "We don't want to impose."

"Impose?" Rocco laughed. "My nephew is here, he has two beautiful friends, no offence Matthew, and we have a beautiful morning. So we go."

Jenny turned to look at Daniel who raised his hands in mock defeat. He and Matthew followed Rocco out to the car. The whole time Rocco never stopped talking to Jenny and Sarah,

"So it is your first visit?"

"Yes," answered Sarah.

"Ah. I have so much to show you. You will love it."

He ushered them inside his car, putting Sarah in first,

"Slide over" he said before ensuring Jenny didn't hit her head and then almost pushing Daniel in as well to fill the back seat. Then he cleared off the front seat for Matthew,

"Lots of space see."

Rocco ran round to the driver's side and sped away, still talking,

"I was going to take the boys out to breakfast and then onto the caves but you all look like you need some sunshine. So we go to Wied iż-Żurrieq."

"Where's that?" Jenny asked Daniel but he did not get a chance to reply.

"The Blue Grotto. You must see this. It is the best time now. You will see, won't they Daniel?"

Once more Daniel had little time to do anything but

agree.

"After, we have breakfast. A nice café nearby. I remember no food before boat ride, hey, Daniel?"

That was a memory Daniel would have preferred everyone forgot. Rocco took Matthew's hand and put it on the steering wheel then turned round to look at his passengers in the back,

"So Daniel you introduce your friends?"

"Jenny and Sarah this is my uncle Rocco."

Rocco shook both of their hands,

"Very good to meet you," he said and then returned his focus to driving but his questions and chatter did not stop. "So you are from the coast, like Daniel, or maybe the city like Matthew?"

"Well we're from Sheffield," said Sarah.

"Ah I went there once. With the steel works?"

"Yes," said Jenny.

"And you are at the university?"

"Yes," they both replied.

"How's the job Matthew, still good, still the same place?"

"Yes," answered Matthew.

There was not a lot of time for anything other than quick answers but it never ceased to impress Daniel how much his uncle retained from his almost one sided conversations.

It took a little over twenty minutes for them to get to Wied iż-Żurrieq and Rocco parked up along the side of the road. The place gave little away as to what it might be or what they would see. There were no bustling crowds, just some local people sitting outside enjoying the morning sun and a calm in the air. Rocco led them round a couple of corners towards the inlet and down a long ramp with wooden battens fixed to it. Ahead of them a line of boats sat in the azure sea. Rocco went over to a local and had a quick discussion before returning to the group.

"Very calm today," said Rocco slapping Daniel's arm, "he'll take us out now."

With that they went down to the water's edge where a couple of men pulled the brightly coloured boat closer to the ramp. They all got in with the man Rocco had spoken to and the other two men shoved the boat on its way. Their helmsman brought the engine to life and they were off.

Jenny turned to Daniel and spoke over the noise of the engine,

"Do you have a problem with boats?"

"I get a little sea sick," said Daniel remembering a couple of unfortunate incidents.

"Are you okay?" asked Jenny.

Daniel smiled at her and nodded.

"No shark sightings recently," said Rocco.

The two girls looked worried. Jenny moved closer to Daniel and Sarah pushed up close to Matthew. Rocco laughed with a glint of mischief in his eyes.

"Are there really sharks?" asked Jenny.

"Yes, but you're safe," said Daniel.

Jenny pressed a little closer to Daniel, despite or perhaps because of his words, which did not go unnoticed by Rocco who let his hand run through the water until they left the inlet and saw the wide open sea ahead of them. As the boat began to pick up speed it was a little bumpy but then it began to almost glide over the water.

The boat turned to port arcing out away from the coastline. They watched the waves smash against the cliffs as they continued towards the Blue Grotto. The water entranced Daniel and he wondered what treasures were hidden beneath. How many of his ancestors had sailed on these very waters? Then in the near distance he saw an arm of rock coming out of the cliff and plunging into the sea. Behind it was a series of caverns. The boat went inside and reduced its power. It was mesmerizing, the cavern's walls had been formed by thousands of years of erosion but seemed as if designed to form the barrel ceiling of some grand hall or great palace. The sunlight bounced off and through the water turning it into every shade of blue imaginable. Daniel encouraged Jenny to put her hand in the water and together they did. The water seemed to turn her hand blue. She had to pull it out of the water to believe it was an optical illusion. It was with great reticence they moved away from each cavern but each and every one was its own particular work of art. In some the water seemed so dark a blue you could imagine the sea went down forever, others were lit up with brilliant phosphorescent colours and the water so clear you could see the sea floor.

The journey back to dry land was quiet. Everyone was content to look at the coastline, the waves, the sea, and the horizon. Back on shore they all thanked their helmsman and walked back up the ramp.

"That was amazing," said Jenny to Daniel.

"Yes it was," he said.

"It was so peaceful and beautiful. I wish we could have stayed longer."

Daniel knew how she felt, for he would have happily stayed in that moment with her, and enjoyed nature's simple majesty for as long as he could.

They arrived back at Rocco's car and he announced,

"Now we eat."

They all got back inside in the same order as before and Rocco sped away once more. There was no time to think or ask where they were going because after a few turns they stopped outside a restaurant.

The others were a little baffled by the short journey but Daniel was simply amused. He had forgotten how Rocco was. Rocco was taking the lead and they all had to play catch up. He went inside the restaurant but it wasn't what they expected. For breakfast it was serving cake, biscuits and processed meat.

Daniel looked at his friends and they all looked a bit uncertain, he overheard Sarah say to Jenny,

"Cake for breakfast?"

Rocco seeing their confusion said,

"It's the most important meal of the day, yes?" he waited for a stirring of agreement and continued. "So why not eat what you like."

Daniel had a sweet tooth and needed no more persuasion and began looking at the cakes and Jenny followed him. Matthew and Sarah took a little more coaxing but Rocco did not take no for an answer and so they all ate cake for breakfast and washed it down with a healthy dose of tea. Rocco was pleased with the progress,

"It was good?"

"Yes," was the resounding answer from all of them.

"So now we carry on?"

Daniel was the first to follow his uncle and the others tagged along. Not certain what could possibly be next? They hopped back into the car and were off once again.

"You know they film many shows here," said Rocco pointing back to the Blue Grotto, "but now I take you to Ħaġar Qim temples,"

The trip only took a few minutes along the coast and as they arrived the greenery gave way to an arid looking dust, out of which rose the limestone pillars of the Megalithic temple.

"It's like Stonehenge," said Sarah.

"Yes but older," said Daniel.

"Ah you remember," said Rocco clearly delighted. "Now go explore."

Rocco remained by the car and Daniel saw him discreetly light a cigarette. They began to explore the structure which consisted of a series of C-shaped rooms called apses. The walls and slabs were hewn out of large blocks of stone. Some had portholes cut through as doorways others seemed to be patterned but all bore evidence of the passage of time. Jenny was fascinated and keen to know more and asked Daniel,

"How old are they?"

"Over three thousand years BC".

It clearly surprised her.

"Not what you expected to see?" asked Daniel.

"No. Not at all. I guess I didn't really know what to expect."

Daniel was pleased and glad he could show her around a bit. Their shared interest and the layout of the temple meant they separated from Matthew and Sarah.

"Malta still surprises me," said Daniel.

"Your family are from here?" asked Jenny.

"My father."

"Your mother?"

"She's English."

"How did they meet?"

"He was in the air force and came to England. How about you? Are your parents from Sheffield?"

"No, I moved there for university but I'm back home in London now."

They walked a little more looking at the monolithic structures.

"You like architecture?" he asked.

"Yes. That was my course."

"Well I think you've come to the right place, there's baroque, gothic revival, megalithic," he said pointing to their surroundings, "neoclassical, renaissance, and vernacular."

"You surprise me." said Jenny quite genuinely.

"Well I don't know what most of it means."

Jenny smiled at him.

"But I'd like to show you some of it. If you'd like?"

"I would, very much so."

If she hadn't been right there at that moment Daniel would have completely over-reacted with joy.

"Ah, there you are," said Rocco, "the others are ready to go."

"So soon?" asked Daniel.

Rocco did not have an answer and so they followed him back to the car where they found a rather bored looking Sarah who on seeing Jenny looked a little guilty.

"It's okay," Jenny said to her.

"Oh my god," Sarah cried jumping from one foot to another, "what was that?" she said pointing.

The others saw a tiny little lizard scurrying past.

"He's harmless," said Rocco, "a little lizard come out to get some sun."

Sarah tried to shrug and shake off the chill the tiny creature had given her.

"So now I take you to the craft village and we get some drinks, maybe more cake?" said Rocco.

The journey to Ta' Qali Crafts Village took a little over twenty minutes with mostly farmland along the way. As they approached the village Rocco pointed out the walled city of Mdina in the distance. The village itself wasn't actually a village at all but an abandoned airfield where the old Nissen huts had been converted and a few new buildings created. At first sight it did not look like much but Daniel knew there was a lot hidden away. Rocco encouraged them all to take a look around.

All around them were lots of different crafts including glass works, potteries, weaving and embroidery, blacksmiths and a few knockoff shops. Daniel was keen to look at the blacksmiths and the suits of armour and Matthew had the same inclination.

"Boys," exclaimed Sarah but was then equally distracted by the leather shops which paraded handbags and purses.

Matthew was so taken with the suits of armour that he bought a miniature one as a souvenir but both he and Daniel really wanted the full sized suit in which the chest panel opened out revealing a drinks bar. Such things were beyond their means and probably any chance of ever having a happy relationship. With that thought in mind Daniel went to find Jenny whilst Matthew tagged along.

They weaved between the hangars and caught sight of them coming out of a shop that was set apart from the others, with large sculptures outside and together they went towards the large glass factory. As soon as they approached they could feel the heat wafting out. The process was intriguing. First they would take a lump of molten glass out of a fiery furnace on a long metal tube. Then they would beat it into shape knocking off the impurities from the glowing red hot glass. Next the glass makers would roll it before they inhaled massive amounts of air which they blew down the tube to make the glass expand. They made it seem as easy as blowing up a balloon. From this stage they could tint the glass with any colour or insert patterns before they quenched it and allowed it to cool further. That was one of the simplest processes for making things like vases but they undertook far more complicated tasks and even something as small as an air bubble in their work could mean it was discarded. The four of them watched in fascination but Daniel's attention was divided between the men forging and sculpting the hot viscous glass and Jenny. For a moment it was as if he was seeing everything anew. Through her eyes the colour of the fiery glass was more intense, every detail was more exact and the forgers seemed to force the glass into their desired shape by pure will power. He snapped back to his own perspective and saw the colour drain from Jenny's face. Daniel moved to support her and asked,

"Are you all right?"

She was disorientated for a moment. Sarah came over looking concerned. Jenny regained her bearings,

"The heat got to me," she said.

Daniel looked for somewhere for her to sit and saw some chairs at the edge of the factory. Sarah took Jenny's other arm and they walked her over to the chairs.

"Sit down," said Sarah.

"I'm okay. Really," said Jenny.

Neither Daniel nor Sarah were entirely convinced but Jenny gave them both a look which told them to stop worrying and she didn't want such a fuss.

"Take your time," said Sarah.

"I'm fine. Go and look around."

Sarah did not move.

"I'll look after her," Daniel told her, "we'll meet you in the shop."

"They'll be okay," said Matthew.

"Go," said Jenny, "we'll be right there."

Sarah took the message and went into the shop with Matthew to begin looking around at the testimonies of the glass workers craft. Jenny remained seated for another minute before she stood up. Her colouring had improved a little but she took Daniel's arm, he wasn't sure if it was out of affection or simply a precaution against falling. They went to join Matthew and Sarah in the air conditioned shop. The transformation from the balls of molten glass they had seen in the factory to what was on the shelves was astounding. The display ranged from the simplest paper weight with glass flowers growing inside it, swans forever swimming, vases and glasses of all shapes, sizes and patterns to sculpted pieces. The cooler air helped Jenny regain her bearings completely.

"I'm much better now," she said to Daniel, "but I'm kind of nervous around all these breakable things. I'd hate to break anything so beautiful," said Jenny.

"I'm sure you wouldn't."

"But to be on the safe side."

"We can go back outside if you like?"

"It might be better."

Daniel stepped over to Matthew,

"We're going to step outside."

"Okay. I think Sarah's buying something. I'll wait for her," said Matthew.

Daniel and Jenny left the shop and the factory and found a shaded spot under a palm tree to sit. Once Jenny was seated Daniel went over to a vending machine and put in a few coins and pushed a couple of buttons. There was the sound a clinking glass as a bottle was dispensed. He repeated the process and then popped the caps off and returned to sit by Jenny.

"Glass bottles," said Jenny.

"I know. It always tastes better than out of the plastic ones."

"Why is that?"

"I don't know. I remember when we were younger they used to give you paper straws too."

"How did that work out?"

"They always disintegrated, but that was part of the fun," said Daniel sipping from the bottle. "Do you feel better?"

"I'm fine," said Jenny, "but thank you."

"It does get pretty hot in there. I couldn't imagine working in that heat all day long."

"It was quite intense."

"I know we didn't spend much time at the temple ruins."

"I understand. Not everyone is interested in history."

Rocco re-joined them.

"You wanted to see more of the temples?" asked Rocco.

"No it was fine," said Jenny not wanting to seem ungracious.

"But you liked the history?"

"Very much. It is quite amazing to think what people accomplished without all of our technology."

Rocco smiled. Daniel saw Matthew and Sarah returning from the glass shop.

"You found something?" asked Rocco.

"Yes," said Sarah showing them the glass dolphin.

"And Matthew?"

Matthew showed Rocco the knight he had bought.

"Very good, so now we go over to the main pottery shop, yes?" asked Rocco.

Rocco waited for Daniel and Jenny to stand up and then they followed him towards the main pottery works. In the shop there were hundreds of varying items, from money pots to oil lamps and novelty items including a pot that looked like a paper bag. Daniel found the idea was strange but could not help stretching forth his hand and touching it to ensure it really was pottery and not paper. Rocco called them all over to see the pottery workshop. Inside the small room was well lit by a window and a light bulb. There was a woman sat behind a potter's wheel who looked up at them. Rocco said something to her in Maltese and she smiled and asked,

"Would you like to try?"

Sarah took one look at all the clay and dirt and shook her head, the potter laughed and offered her an apron,

"To protect your clothes."

"No, I'm sorry but thank you," she said looking at Jenny for reassurance.

Rocco wasn't about to give up on any of them and he pushed Daniel forward. He wasn't sure but he was willing to give it a go. The potter cut the pot she was making off the wheel and put it on the table behind her for firing later. She threw down a fresh lump of clay and stood up so Daniel could take a seat. Daniel stepped forward and sat down on the stool. The potter showed him where to press the pedal which made the table turn and she instructed him,

"Put your hands here and draw it upwards."

Daniel did as he was told and the clay began to rise.

"Good," said the potter, "now put your thumbs inside."

He did as he was instructed and saw the beginning of a lip form as the cylinder opened out into a primitive shape. The others were impressed and cheered him on a little but it was too soon. The clay started to lean lopsidedly and thinned too much on one side and then it collapsed. Daniel slowed the wheel down to have a look at his creation. It looked more like a plate with a bowl in the centre than a pot. On seeing Daniel's effort Matthew backed away saying,

"I think I'll leave it to the professionals."

The potter looked at Jenny and asked,

"Would you like to try?"

"I don't want to embarrass myself."

Daniel looked at her and she tracked his eyes to his sad effort.

"You must try," said Rocco, "or maybe you like to try together. Like in the film, Ghost."

Matthew and Sarah both stifled a laugh as Jenny and Daniel both turned bright red. Daniel stood up and quickly exited to try and avoid any further embarrassing frames of reference. He tried not to look at Jenny as he left the room but he couldn't help it and his face went redder still. Jenny did not know which way to turn but they were all looking at her and so she stepped into the potter's room and sat down. The potter placed an apron over her and then removed Daniel's creation and threw a fresh lump of clay on the table. She whispered something in Jenny's ear which Daniel did not hear and then she helped her to start the shape. From there Jenny began to extend it upwards and began hollowing it out into the shape of a bowl before bringing it back in and pulling up the neck of the vase. When she was finished she slowed the table down. They were all surprised. It looked like a proper vase. The potter cut it from the table and placed it on the rack to be fired, she turned and looked at Daniel and Rocco,

"You see. It takes a woman's touch."

Rocco slapped Daniel on the back as his consolation prize and spoke to the potter in Maltese before addressing his little group,

"Now I take you back for the siesta. Then this evening you all come for tea."

Outside the pottery workshop Daniel and Jenny used the exterior tap to clean their hands and Daniel asked,

"What did she whisper to you?"

Jenny smiled and said coyly,

"I can't tell you."

Then she walked back to the car air drying her hands as she went.

Rocco dropped all four of them back at the hotel and told them once more that they had to come to tea. With that he zipped away to start his siesta. The four of them stood in the hotel lobby not certain what to do next as none of them were used to siestas.

"I think most places close?" asked Matthew.

"Quite a few apart from some tourist things and restaurants," said Daniel.

They lingered and in that silence Daniel thought back to the car, and how Jenny's hand and his had touched. How they had linked fingers, as if no one would notice the little prelude to holding her hand. Her hand seemed so delicate, so fragile and small compared to his, each of her fingers so slight and soft. He realised his attention was drifting and so he came back to the present.

"We had better check on Phillip and Lisa," said Daniel.

"I'll check the room," said Sarah.

"I'll check ours," said Matthew.

With that they went and left Daniel and Jenny together in the lobby.

"I guess they're doing the checking," said Daniel.

"I think Sarah is trying to give us a little time alone."

Daniel had not felt nervous until she had said that.

"I had a good time today," said Jenny.

"I'm glad."

"It was kind of your uncle to show us around like that."

"I think he likes to."

Daniel was trying to think of more to say but his mind was blank. They waited together in silence for a long minute.

"I hope you will come for tea," said Daniel hoping Jenny would agree.

"I'm not sure we should."

"You have to," said Daniel not knowing why she would have to, "Rocco will be upset if you don't come."

"We'll have to find out how Lisa and your brother are first."

Daniel was about to agree with her when he saw William, his grandfather, enter the hotel. He went to meet him.

"Grandad."

"Daniel, my boy. Ah the sun agrees with you," said William looking with some difficulty through his thick glasses.

"What are you doing here? I thought you would be taking a siesta?"

"Your gran takes the siesta. Sometimes me to, but

most days I walk."

"You walked here from Valletta?" said Daniel expressing his concern given his grandfather's age and the heat.

"Of course. I often do. Not perhaps as much as I used to, but still. And today we go to Rocco's for tea, so he brings your gran and drives us back."

His grandfather never ceased to amaze him. He was approaching his nineties and nothing seemed to stop him.

"Where is your brother?"

"We were just trying to find that out," said Daniel glancing back to Jenny.

William followed his look and saw Jenny waiting patiently and gave his grandson an inquisitive look.

"I'm sorry I should have introduced you. Grandad this is Jenny. Jenny my grandfather, William," said Daniel feeling awkward.

William's face lit up with a big smile and he took Jenny's hand and shook it vigorously.

"Ah, very glad to meet you."

"Pleased to meet you."

"You're a very beautiful girl," said William. "Why didn't you tell us you had such a pretty girlfriend?"

Daniel blushed and tried to explain,

"Jenny's a guest here too."

"Oh, so you aren't together?" William asked sounding disappointed.

"Well we're friends," said Jenny.

"That's a good start," said William.

Matthew and Sarah walked across to them from the lift.

"Hello," said Matthew.

William shook Sarah's hand with equal vigour.

"Another friend?" asked William.

"I'm Sarah."

"This is good, so many new people," said William. "And you are all enjoying a holiday?"

"Yes," said Sarah.

"It is good. And Phillip?" William asked again.

"Apparently he's at the beach," said Matthew.

"With Lisa," added Sarah.

"They are there now?" asked William.

"Yes," Matthew answered.

"Oh they will be like sardines in a tin," William chuckled, "much better to go early, hey Daniel?"

"I think so but you know Phillip."

"Ah yes," said William, "so we take some tea here and then we all go to Rocco's. Yes?"

Daniel wondered if there was any room for debate but his grandfather sat down and waited for everyone else to join him. There was an empty seat near Jenny but Daniel did not know if he should sit next to her, or opposite her by his grandfather, or remain standing. He saw the way Jenny looked at him and even his own grandfather seemed to be telling him to sit next to her. This was all such new territory for him. Only in his dreams could he have imagined bringing such a beautiful girl to meet his family but now here he was with Jenny and nothing could have made him happier at that moment.

William regaled them with stories of how life used to be in Malta and kept them all spellbound and as if to add to the magic several pots of tea kept appearing. None of them knew that there was a drinks service in the lobby lounge but someone kept bringing them until it was time for them to leave. William sent Daniel outside to see if Rocco had arrived and sure enough he saw his uncle waiting for them.

"So now we go," said William looking at them all. He struggled to get up from the low seat.

Both Sarah and Jenny went to his aid which only delighted him further. Once William was standing he kept hold of both their arms to steady himself. Jenny turned to Daniel,

"Are you sure we should come with you?"

William, still holding on to them both with a strength that belied his age, told them,

"We are now all friends, yes?"

"Yes," they both replied.

"And friends are like family. So-"

"So we go," said Jenny.

"Good you understand," said William.

They all went out to Rocco's car where there was an evident problem. They could not all fit.

"I go and come back," said Rocco.

"I can walk," said Daniel.

"You remember the way?" asked Rocco.

"Of course. I'll be ten minutes behind you.'

"You're sure?"

"Yes," said Daniel.

Everyone else got in the car except Jenny,

"I'll walk too," she said.

"Ah I see," said Rocco with that same glint of mischief in his eye from earlier in the day and with that he pulled away.

"You didn't have to walk," said Daniel.

"I wanted to," she said taking his hand.

They walked along the coast for a few minutes before cutting inland to cross to the other side of Sliema. The buildings changed rapidly from those on the coast. The hotels and tourist traps gave way to something that resembled more of the old town that Daniel's grandfather had told them about. Buildings were thin and tall, with enclosed balconies on many, and bundles of wires above from modernisation. The windows and doors were highly decorated with ornate iron patterns over the glass and door knockers of all different kinds from lions and crosses to dolphins and cherubs. As they walked Daniel tried to imagine how it had been almost three quarters of a century earlier, when his grandfather was their age. How his grandparents might have walked those same streets together just as he was with Jenny, and how they were visiting the same places they had when they had courted. He wished he could show her the whole island.

Daniel took his time as they got closer to Rocco's house, partly because he wanted to stay with Jenny but also because things had changed in the two years since he was last there. He recognised enough of the older buildings to be assured they were in the right place and then he saw Rocco's house. When he pushed the button on the intercom it crackled loudly. Daniel spoke into the box,

"Hello. It's us."

The intercom buzzed and then the door clicked unlocked and they went inside. On the ground floor there were a couple of doors off to the sides and a large three storey staircase at the end of the hallway. They heard someone moving at the top of the stairs,

"Daniel," called his aunt Charlotte, "come up."

They went up to the top floor where Rocco was standing behind his wife Charlotte who placed both hands on Daniel's shoulders.

"Let me have a good look at you," she said and then

kissed him on both cheeks and gave him a big hug.

"You're too thin," said Charlotte squeezing him.

Daniel watched as his aunt moved to look at Jenny and kissed her on the cheek. Uncertain of what to do Jenny backed away.

"Both cheeks, always both cheeks" said Charlotte kissing her on the other cheek.

Jenny did her best to accept the warm greeting.

"Now let's eat. Yes? You're both too thin. I have your favourites."

Charlotte took them to the living room where the snacks were being served ahead of the main meal. The room was full of Daniel's relatives. There were aunts and uncles, many cousins and his grandparents along with Matthew and Sarah. It was a chaotic scene at first with so many introductions and questions. Everyone wanted to know everything all at the same time. It soon settled down as Charlotte called them to the dining table which she had lavishly prepared with an array of food and drink. So began an evening of good food and even better company. The conversation flowed with stories of the past couple of years, of who was getting married, how many new children there were and a bit of politics to stir it all up.

After the first course no one was a stranger and the only sadness was for those who weren't there that evening including Phillip. Daniel felt bad that his brother was not there, even though he knew he would be having fun somewhere, he actually missed him. Not that he would ever admit that to him. Jenny noticed his brief malaise and softly rubbed his back and smiled at him. Her smile lifted him beyond words. With that push he re-engaged with his family. It was rare to see so many family members all together at the same time but it felt good. Different to how he usually felt with people, or crowds, or even just by himself. This time there wasn't any need for pre-defined speeches and Daniel was glad his grandparents saw him with Jenny, more so because he felt like himself again, as if all the walls he had built up in becoming an adult had fallen away and he was able to be himself. Able to live in that moment, a moment of perfect happiness.

The joy and laughter of a loving family and good food took them through the night until fatigue began to overtake them a few at a time. Daniel's grandparents were the first to depart, giving their love to everyone and making him promise to visit them in a couple of days' time before Rocco drove them home. Slowly more and more people left until only Daniel, Jenny, Matthew and Sarah remained with Charlotte who delighted in having her special guests to herself for a while. She told them of all the places they should visit, Dingli cliffs, Marsaxlokk, but avoid the rest of Pretty Bay as it wasn't so pretty any more but visit Gozo, especially Gozo if they had the time. Charlotte did not want to let them go but Rocco returned to give them a ride back to the hotel. When they left Charlotte was as sad as could be for not knowing if she would see her nephew and his sweet friends again. Daniel tried to reassure her that they would see each other again before they left and next time Phillip would be with them but still the goodbyes were far longer than the introductions and much more difficult.

After waving goodbye to Rocco at the hotel they went inside exhausted from the day. Sarah excused herself and retired for the evening leaving the three of them. Matthew proposed that they might have a nightcap in the bar. That night there had been a singer performing, and she was approaching the concluding numbers of her act. The three of them sat on a settee against a wall and watched and listened. The singer was dressed in a long blue dress, without sleeves but with a high neck. Her face was deeply tanned and she wore light blue eye shadow. She was accompanied by a pianist and a couple of guitarists. The bar was still quite full, a testimony to her talents. More so because most people were dancing together. Mostly they simply swayed and turned a little with the music and the singing but there were a few couples who were more comfortable with performing. Daniel wondered if he could dance at all. He doubted it but when he looked at Jenny he wanted to. He wanted to dance with her very much. Then he saw his brother and Lisa. They both appeared to have caught a little too much sun and they weren't so much dancing as half falling asleep standing up next to each other.

Daniel looked to Matthew and Jenny with an expression that simply said, not again. Jenny burst out laughing. Daniel got up ready to be his brother's care taker once again. Jenny was still laughing and it became infectious fortunately for them no one else could hear their laughter over the sound of the music as no one else would have understood it. Daniel went over to his brother and managed to stir him long enough that he and Matthew escorted them off the dance floor and up to their suite. Once again they decided to leave them together, this time in the end room. Matthew stayed behind to watch over them whilst Daniel chaperoned Jenny. When they reached her room Daniel paused outside the door as she opened it. He did not go in but he very much wanted to. She stepped inside and waited for a moment before turning to face him.

"I had a lovely day. Thank you," she said.

Daniel really did not want that to be the end and she read his mind, at least the best part of it.

"Perhaps we could spend the morning together?"

His feelings of joy were soon intensified as she leaned forwards and kissed him softly on the cheek. Daniel felt his legs tremble.

"Both cheeks, yes?" she said to him before kissing his other cheek as tenderly as she had the first.

"Goodnight," she whispered.

If the door frame had not been there Daniel would have fallen and it took every bit of concentration he could muster for him to reply,

"Goodnight."

Jenny closed the door softly leaving Daniel standing in the corridor desperately wanting her to open the door and kiss him one more time.

## CHAPTER FOUR

Jenny leaned against the door. Was it hot in here she wondered and looked over at the air conditioning which was gusting. She kept thinking things over in her mind, all the places they had been, everything everyone had said, and the smallest moments she and Daniel had shared. Was she going mad? Imagining things that weren't real to create a fantasy? Why had she kissed him? It was only on the cheek, she told herself but that did not stop her from wanting to open the door again and asking Daniel to enter, to stay with her, but she knew she couldn't. It would not be right she told herself over and over but still Jenny kept thinking of him. It took a lot of effort for her to wrench herself away from the door but the whole time she wished Daniel would return. She hoped and listened for a knock on the door but there was none and Jenny truly did not know what she would do if he did come back. It seemed as if they had only just met.

They had only just met she told herself but she didn't care. She wanted to see him again now, she did not want to wait till the morning. But she would she told herself. Jenny slipped off her shoes as she entered the bedroom and then went into the bathroom to turn the shower on. She undressed and stepped under the shower head. The heat from the shower filled the room with steam as she carefully washed her hair. For a second Jenny worried that she might not hear the door and so she quickly finished and shut off the shower. She wrapped a large towel around herself and began to dry her hair. The noise of the hair drier sounded deafening. She turned it off and listened. There was no knocking on the door and she told herself that she was being quite silly. With that Jenny finished drying her hair, put on her nightgown and lay down on the bed, not wanting to fall asleep right away. Jenny closed her eyes and asked herself out loud,

"What are you doing? Stop it right now."

But she could not stop thinking about him and she could not wait for the morning to come. Her mind began to swirl and soon she was caught in her dreams.

The sunrise began to leak through the thin curtains and pulled Jenny out her dreams and with the dawn she got up, slipped out of her nightgown, and freshened up attempting to tame her hair. As soon as she felt she looked respectable, or at least not a complete mess she finished dressing and glanced at the clock. It was still far too early, an utterly uncivilized hour but she was up and ready to go. She drew back the thin curtains and basked for a moment as the first morning rays of sun warmed her. Thinking that she did not want to waste a moment, she went downstairs. The lobby was completely silent, without even the night porter present. The only person there was Daniel. He was slumped in one of the lounge chairs. How long had he been there? Jenny asked herself. It was clear he had not slept much if at all but on seeing Jenny he threw his fatigue aside and walked over to her.

"Good morning," he said warmly.

"Good morning."

"I didn't expect anyone else to be up for several hours."

"Neither did I. But…"

"But here we are."

Jenny looked at him, his morning stubble made him seem more rugged, more handsome she thought. She stood in front of him ready and willing to follow him wherever he wanted to go.

"I thought we could take a bus into Valletta," said Daniel.

"Okay," Jenny replied.

They left the hotel and walked to the bus stop where they waited for a few minutes. Jenny asked herself if there would be a bus that early in the morning but soon enough one arrived and it was nearly empty. They hopped on board and the bus continued its first journey of the day, following the coast through Gzira and into Ta' Xbiex where they caught glimpses of the ambassadorial residences and mansions. Jenny saw one house which was covered in a vine with brilliant purple flowers, others had elaborate carvings, and dramatic staircases leading to the fortified front entrances. She was quite engrossed in the view when Daniel said,

"Come on we're going to hop off here."

She looked around and saw Valletta a little way off in the distance.

"Are we there?" she asked.

"Not quite. I wanted to show you somewhere else first."

They got off the bus and Jenny followed Daniel as they walked around the coast until the footpath diverged from the road. Daniel continued walking along the road and up a hill where he stopped outside a gate set into the large limestone walls.

"Where are we?" asked Jenny.

Daniel opened the gate and she saw a long garden filled with palm trees and all kinds of local flora that she had never seen before.

"Can we go in?"

"Yes."

They stepped through the gate into the hidden garden and followed the long path which gradually opened to reveal multiple levels interconnected by ramps and steps. The stairs led down to the lower ramparts of the garden that appeared to be embedded in the gigantic walled fortifications. Daniel continued to guide her upwards through to the top level of the garden. At first it seemed that the top part was in ruins with hardly any plants and gravel covering the ground. Without the protection of the garden's walls it was windy. Then Jenny saw the sentry box.

"You'd better hold on to your hat," Daniel said as he began to climb the steps to the small tower which jutted out from the fortress.

Jenny followed him with the wind pushing them back almost as if it wanted to hide a secret. They entered the turret like sentry post and from its windows they had a panoramic view out over Sliema, Pieta and Marsamxett harbour, Valletta and the countryside in the distance. The wind kept pushing them but Daniel stood behind Jenny, bracing her, as he pointed out,

"That's our hotel in Sliema and over there is my grandparent's flat in Valletta."

The openings of the sentry tower framed each view into perfect portraits, which Jenny tried to absorb before the wind seemed to push them away once more. They returned through the garden, past a quaint conservatory with its frame painted a deep green and hiding away a multitude of potted plants. Once outside the garden on the road Jenny looked back at the walls which kept their secret so well.

They walked along the road a short distance before they found another footpath and followed it through Floriana along the mall, which was a long promenade, until they reached the main bus terminus outside the walls to Valletta. The terminus seemed chaotic with ancient old English buses repainted yellow and orange circling around the mammoth Triton Fountain. It was already bustling with people boarding, disembarking and weaving through the maze. Jenny had to take Daniel's hand for fear of being separated and lost. Her worries soon dissipated as they approached a large bridge leading to the gateway into the city through the fortified walls. The bridge itself had stalls on both sides, all selling food which filled the air with a sweet aroma. Jenny lingered and looked at several of the stalls, with the sweet breads and biscuits.

"I know of a good place, it is nearby," Daniel told her.

Jenny kind of half shook her head, sure that the food on any one of those stalls would be delicious,

"I didn't think I was hungry till I smelled the food," she said.

"I promise you'll like it and if not we can come right

back."

"Okay then," she said half sad.

They left the food stalls behind and as they continued over the bridge Jenny caught a glimpse of the massive trench below them as they passed through the city gate. She gave the food stalls one last look but as they entered the city itself she was compelled to take in her surroundings which began with a large court area.

"This is Freedom Square," said Daniel, "a lot of it was rebuilt during the sixties."

Looking around Jenny could see the mix of styles. Some of the buildings appeared ancient, some perhaps might be considered eyesores and others appeared to be little but ruins. Daniel tracked her eye movements which landed on a ruin.

"That was the old opera house. It was destroyed during the Second World War," he told her.

"Why did they never rebuild it?"

"It seems to be a complicated matter. Come on let's get a bite to eat."

They crossed over a road and into the main pedestrianized shopping area. As they continued along Republic Street Jenny did not know where to look. The high street was bustling with people, there were all kinds of shops, and the architecture constantly impressed her. It felt like a city of surprises, devoid of the endless chain shops and restaurants that dominated back home. If she hadn't felt so terribly hungry she would have stopped at every other, no every single shop certain that she would find something new in each one. Daniel turned off the high street and she followed him. Within a dozen steps she could smell a bakery. The scent of bread and pastries filled the air and was even more divine than the food stalls they had passed minutes ago. The bakery was not quite what she had expected. There did not appear to be a shop, as such, more a kiosk window in a building. There was a selection of goods displayed in the cabinet window and a healthy queue of people which they joined.

"Do you know what they sell?" asked Jenny.

"Some things but I want you to try a local pastry. If that's okay?"

"I trust you."

Daniel expressed a little mock worry with the responsibility and they continued to move along with the line. As they got closer Jenny heard people ordering but she couldn't understand what was being said.

"Do you understand them?"

"Not as much as I would like," said Daniel with the faintest hint of regret.

The line moved along and Jenny saw a middle aged man with a thinning head of hair serving. He glanced at them and decided they were not locals. He spoke to Daniel in Maltese. On not getting a response the man tried to summon his best English, which amounted to gesticulating with his hands at the bakery's offerings.

"Erba pastizzi," Daniel said awkwardly and acutely aware of his linguistic shortcomings.

The baker's face lit up and he handed Daniel a bag, which he passed to Jenny whilst he paid. Whatever was in the bag was smouldering hot. They left the bakery and Jenny peaked inside the bag,

"Is it a Cornish Pasty?"

"It's a cheesecake, well a cheese pastry."

Daniel took them to a tiny park with little more than some swings and a seesaw.

"Your seat," said Daniel steadying a swing in an

attempt at gallantry.

Jenny took her seat on the swing and handed Daniel the bag which he opened for her. She took one of the pastizzi which was still extremely hot. Daniel sat down on the swing next to her and took one out for himself.

"Here's to your first Maltese cheesecake," he said.

They made a little toast by bumping the pastries together and then Jenny took a small and cautious bite. Steam escaped and she had to wait a minute before it was cool enough to try a little more. On her second bite she discovered the ricotta cheese, but it was not quite like anything she had tasted before. With each bite she enjoyed it a little more. Nearing the end she realised that she had flakes of pastry all over lap. She looked at Daniel who had the same problem and was brushing the crumbs away.

"What other tricks do you have up your sleeve?"

Daniel offered her another pastizz and said,

"Well I guess I'd better not introduce you to Kinnie just yet."

"Who is Kinnie?"

"It's a local soft drink, but something of an acquired taste."

"What does it taste like?"

Daniel was stumped. He had no way to describe it.

"I'll guess you'll have to try it."

"Do you like it?"

Daniel's mouth puckered and he shook his head,

"No."

"But you want me to try it?"

"There has to be a first time for everything, right?"

"Sure, but maybe not today, okay?"

"That's okay. I think I have another idea. How about

a drink with a view unless you'd prefer to stay here and play on the swings?"

Jenny gently punched him on the arm and felt like a little girl, who had no idea how to express her emotions beyond rough housing with a boy. She rocked her legs back and forth and swung for a few minutes in defiance before jumping off.

"What are we waiting for?" she asked Daniel.

"Follow me then," he said.

Even though the city was mostly laid out in a grid Jenny lost track of any sense of direction as Daniel took corner after corner. He led her up long streets and narrow alleys with heavily eroded stairs and down again on the other side. They were going faster and faster with Daniel calling out to her places of interest, Manoel Theatre, the shopping centre, the Palace of the Grand Master and St. John's Co-Cathedral. She had no idea what some of the places were but she ran along with him, past the National Museum of Archaeology and the church of St. Catherine until Daniel stopped out of breath.

"Castille Place," he said breathing heavily.

Jenny had no idea of the significance of the name. In fact compared to some of the places they had been past it seemed a strange place to stop but when Daniel had caught his breath he took her hand and led her past a hotel and towards a gateway. There were several horse drawn carriages, known as karozzin, waiting near the gate and she wanted to make a fuss of all the horses but Daniel steered her away from them,

"I'd like to show you the garden," said Daniel.

Reluctantly she walked away from the horses. The gateway to the garden did not reveal much and she wondered if this could be as incredible as the first one he had shown her. Either way it did not matter as she was enjoying their time together. They passed through the gateway.

"This is the Upper Barrakka," Daniel told her. "It is one of my favourite places."

As she looked around it seemed very pleasant. There was an abundance of pretty coloured flowers, well-manicured hedges and trees and a simple little fountain. There appeared to be a few statues scattered around and a lot of archways that almost looked like an aqueduct but in truth Jenny could not quite figure out why he was so excited to bring her there.

"Will you close your eyes?" he asked.

Jenny looked at him a little unsure and asked, "Why?"

"I really want to show you something through those arches but I don't want you to see it until we're right there."

"All right," she said with a hint of hesitance, "but don't let me walk into anything."

"I won't. I promise but you have to keep your eyes shut."

"Okay then," she said and put her hand over her eyes.

Daniel put his hands on her shoulders and guided her slowly and steadily further into the garden and through the archways.

"Now put out your hand, there's a metal railing directly ahead of you."

She did as he said and took hold of the railing.

"Now open your eyes."

It took her a moment to refocus. At first everything was a blue blur and then it came into focus.

"The Grand Harbour," he said.

Jenny was too stunned for words. She was stood at the highest point of the city walls looking out over a vast harbour with the Mediterranean Sea to her left and the three cities on the other side of the bay. It dwarfed anything she had ever seen before. All she could do was look at the panorama from left to right and back again. She could not believe that mankind could have ever created such an amazing place. The reflections of the cities reached across the harbour and in the water there were all kinds of ships and boats. When Daniel pointed out an enormous cruise liner docked at the port she could not believe she had not seen it and then she saw Valletta's sea front below her too. For a long time she stood there looking. At first the expanse of the harbour appeared static but the longer she looked the more she saw all the facets of life teaming around it. There were cars in the cities in the distance, people walking appearing as small as ants, the boats moved through the harbour hardly disturbing the sea which rippled and shimmered with light. Above them birds flew from one end of the harbour to the other effortlessly in a few minutes, a journey that would take a person an hour.

"It is beautiful," she said turning to hug Daniel.

She was exceptionally happy that she had been there with Daniel. It was so tranquil and quiet despite the people around them.

"I never want to leave," said Jenny.

"I never want you to."

Jenny was completely wrapped up in his arms and wanted to kiss him but she did not dare and so she rested her head against his chest and looked back out over the Grand Harbour. She could hear and feel his heartbeat. He held her a little tighter and in that moment she forgot everything about herself, she felt they belonged together. It was meant to be. It was all that she could ever have wanted. Only reality could break them apart and the truth was they could not stay there forever. They lingered and continued looking at the view, after fetching a drink from the little round kiosk in the garden. Eventually they had to turn from the Grand Harbour and leave the Upper Barrakka behind. They did so having fallen a little more in love with Malta and with each other.

They caught a bus back to Sliema from the terminus. As Jenny gazed out of the window she felt as if she was watching their morning in reverse, passing back by the places they had been earlier. Sometimes she would catch Daniel's reflection in the glass, superimposed over the landscape as if he was a part of the place. If she could not feel him sat next to her, his hand in hers then she might have thought it all nothing but a daydream. It was only as they came to their stop and began to walk back to the hotel that her thoughts turned from Daniel.

"Do you think they noticed we were gone?"

"I don't know. I didn't even think about it."

"What time is it?"

"Hardly gone ten."

"Really?"

"Yes."

"I bet they're only getting up now."

In fact they found that Sarah and Matthew had been up for an hour and were waiting in the lobby not quite certain what to do.

"Sorry," said Jenny.

"We were up early and went for a morning walk," said Daniel.

"That's okay. We were trying to figure out what to do

with the day," said Matthew.

"How's Phillip?" asked Daniel.

"Coming around, slowly," said Matthew.

"Well I think I'll go and rouse him," said Daniel, "and then we could head to Mellieha Bay."

"Where's that?" asked Sarah.

"The beach," replied Daniel.

"That would be good," said Sarah. "We'll get ready."

When they were all reunited they waited for the bus to arrive. Jenny looked over at Daniel, and then over to his brother who was sat hand in hand with Lisa on the wall, attempting to turn the page of his book with one hand. Matthew and Sarah were sat, talking, on one of the benches close by. It pleased Jenny to see her friends enjoying themselves, living in the moment. She questioned herself whether she could do the same with Daniel. Did she have the right to seize a moment of happiness, even if it was fleeting? Her question would have to wait for an answer as the bus arrived and they all began to board. Sarah beckoned Jenny to sit with her, whilst Lisa sat down waiting for Phillip, and Matthew and Daniel took the row in front of her. Phillip was the last to get on as he put his book back into his bag. Unfortunately for him the driver was in a hurry and began to pull away before he had a foothold. Phillip began to run whilst holding onto the door handles and tried to jump up the step and into the bus but he did not make it. The bus began to pick up speed and Phillip was shouting at the bus driver who completely ignored him. Jenny was concerned but she saw Daniel spring into action. He braced himself in the open door and grabbed Phillip's arm to pull him up and into the bus. With his brother's help Phillip managed to get his feet on the step and pull himself on board and proceeded to give the bus driver a death stare. The driver ignored him and sped on with the door remaining open to provide ventilation against the rising heat.

Phillip sat down next to Lisa. Matthew turned around, "Are you okay?"

"Yes, no thanks to that blasted mad man," said Phillip loudly.

"They just don't like you," said Matthew.

"I know they bloody well don't."

Daniel turned and looked at Jenny and Sarah,

"This isn't the first problem he's had with the local transport. Last time we were here he fell off a bus as it pulled away."

"I don't know what he did to the bus drivers in this country but he must have really annoyed them," said Matthew.

Jenny saw Phillip grimace, clearly still angry, but Lisa was consoling him. He had over an hour to cool off and that hour seemed like one of the longest journeys she could have imagined. It was getting hotter and hotter and she did not like being apart from Daniel. All they could do was exchange glances and wait till they arrived. When they did, they all made sure that Phillip was the first off the bus. The beach was already busy with people lined up neatly sunbathing or, she thought, like sardines in a tin, as William had put it. There were all kinds of beach and water activities going on with people playing games on the beach, swimming, windsurfing, parasailing and water-skiing. With so many people already there Phillip nominated himself to find a good spot and expected the others to follow him. When he had found an area to his satisfaction he sent Matthew and Daniel to fetch chairs and parasols. Jenny, Sarah and Lisa began to lay out some towels and decided that they should fetch some refreshments. When they returned with the drinks they found the chairs set up with Daniel and Matthew setting up a few parasols. Phillip was firmly planted in a chair, book in hand. Lisa sat next to him concerned that he was still brooding over his bad start to the day. Jenny and Sarah offered Daniel and Matthew a drink and together they finished setting up their little beach encampment. Daniel looked out towards the sea and asked,

"Does anyone want to go for a swim?"

"I might go in up to my ankles," said Matthew.

"It's quite shallow," said Daniel reassuring him.

"We'll go," said Jenny and Sarah as they stripped down to their bathing costumes.

Jenny could not help but watch as Daniel changed. He was toned in a good way, and she noticed he had a couple of scars, one on his abdomen, and the other on his leg. She wanted to touch them. He tried to block the one on his stomach.

"Don't be embarrassed," said Jenny removing his hand and placing her own over the mark. "We all have scars."

She smiled at him and he lowered his guard and took her hand all the way down to the water. Sarah and Matthew followed, though Matthew had only removed his shoes. At the water's edge she and Daniel tested the water. At first it felt a little cool but as they waded a little further it became more pleasant. Matthew was very slow and taking his time and Sarah had to ask,

"What's the matter?"

"Nothing," said Matthew, "but I can't swim."

Despite that he went in up to his knees before deciding that was far enough. Daniel kept going but warned them,

"It stays pretty shallow for a while but then there are a few steep drop offs."

"Maybe I'll just swim in the shallow bit then," said Jenny.

Daniel stopped and turned to wait for her.

"You and Sarah carry on," said Jenny.

He resisted but the sea was calling him onwards and so he continued to wade further out. Sarah stopped by Jenny,

"Are you okay?"

"I'm fine. A little tired that's all. Now go before he gets away from you."

Jenny watched as Sarah followed Daniel until both of them found deeper water and submerged themselves to swim. She paddled back towards Matthew to keep him company.

"I wish I had learned to swim," Matthew told her.

"I'm sure it isn't too late," said Jenny.

Matthew continued paddling and Jenny followed him.

"I'm glad you and Sarah are getting along."

"She's a nice girl."

"Only a nice girl?" quizzed Jenny in a friendly fashion.

Matthew smiled at her and answered,

"I think I'm a little too old for her."

"You're not much older than Daniel are you?"

"Over a decade."

"Well, I'm surprised," she confessed.

"Still it seems Phillip and Lisa are getting along."

They both looked back to the beach to where Phillip and Lisa were sunbathing.

"I think Lisa gets along well with most men," Jenny bit her lip, she thought that sounded a little too mean. "I didn't mean it like that."

"That's all right. I think I know what you meant. Phillip is the same way. That is with women of course, not men, or bus drivers for that matter."

Jenny turned to see Daniel and Sarah still swimming in the distance, diving down from time to time to search the seabed beneath them. She realised she was staring too long and looked back at Matthew.

"Maybe I should ask you about Daniel?" he said.

She felt herself blush, but hoped that he could not tell under the intense sun.

"He's a good man. I know I'm biased but he's different from his brother. Not that Phillip's bad." Matthew forced himself to stop talking.

"I know," said Jenny.

Truly she felt it in her heart that he was different. Different from anyone else she had ever known. Even at that moment she could feel how much she cared for him and it frightened her and amazed her all at the same time. She sighed far more audibly than she had intended but Matthew did not seem to notice. He went a little deeper into the water, until he felt and clearly looked uncomfortable and said to Jenny,

"Sometimes it is good to take a risk beyond your comfort zone."

It seemed to her that his message could not be any clearer and her resistance was crumbling. Once more she gazed at Daniel. The last thing she wanted was to hurt him or get hurt herself but she did not know if she even dared to take such a risk.

When the swimmers and paddlers were back ashore they went to a nearby café to fetch lunch for all of them. The food, warm weather and the locale lifted all of their spirits, even Phillip emerged from the doldrums, though he soon returned to his book.

"Hey, no more reading," said Lisa but Phillip only glanced at her. "Let's go for a swim."

"No, I've just eaten. You can't swim after eating."

"That's not true," insisted Lisa.

"Maybe in a while," said Phillip.

Jenny watched Lisa as she began digging out the sand behind Phillip's chair and felt that it probably was not the best idea but it was too late. The sand crumbled and the chair collapsed into the hole jolting Phillip. He dropped his book which Lisa picked up.

"Hey, give that back."

Lisa shook her head and ran off saying,

"Come and get it."

Phillip half ran after her but Lisa ran a loop around him back to the others. She threw his book to Daniel and then ran back towards the sea. Phillip came back and saw his book in Daniel's hands. He clearly thought about taking his book back but on seeing Lisa in the sea decided on another course of action. They all watched them splash around in the sea with Lisa determined to overpower Phillip and knock him down and eventually she succeeded.

Whilst Phillip and Lisa were playing Matthew and Sarah both rested under the blazing sun. Feeling the heat on her skin Jenny looked at Daniel and said,

"Would you put some sun lotion on my back?"

Daniel put the book down and fetched some lotion. Jenny turned over onto her front. She felt his hands begin to apply the lotion and she removed the shoulder straps to ensure he could cover her whole back. The lotion was cool but his hands were warm and his touch was gentle, almost timid. It was as if he was afraid his caresses were wrong. When he had finished Jenny rolled onto her front and as she sat up her bathing suit fell down a little. She caught it before it revealed anything but she saw Daniel's eyes flash down to her chest and back up again and he held his breath. Was this enough of a risk she asked herself. They both remained staring at each other quite uncertain of what to do when Phillip and Lisa came back and both slumped into their chairs. Jenny wanted a chance to be alone with Daniel so she could tell him everything that was on her mind.

"Would you like to take a walk?" she asked him.

"Sure," said Daniel.

They walked along the beach away from the others. Jenny was thinking about everything that had brought them to that point and how much more she wanted but she kept telling herself that it should never happen. With every step they took she felt herself burning with desire to risk more, to make herself utterly vulnerable to him and to live entirely for the moment. There did not seem anyway she could tell him how she was feeling and so she stopped and looked out over the water. In the distance she saw someone parasailing. The boat pulled the parachute through the air. It seemed reckless, a little crazy to do such a thing.

"Do you want to have a go?" Daniel asked following her gaze.

"I don't think so. It looks terrifying," she said. "Do you want to?"

It was clear he did before she even finished asking the question.

"I really don't think I could do it," said Jenny, "it looks dangerous."

"We could do it in tandem?"

She asked herself if that was the answer she had been waiting for but she truly did not know.

"Take a risk together," said Daniel.

Jenny knew that Sarah would tell her not to do it. Lisa would probably have already been up there but this was her decision. Her risk to take.

"Okay then. Let's do it," she said still uncertain.

They made their way over to where the parasailing was organised and booked it. There was only a short wait before they were both being harnessed up to the parachute. For a moment Jenny had second thoughts. Was this the kind of risk she really wanted to take? Being pulled into the air attached to a parachute seemed more foolhardy than anything. As the final checks were made she became rather more conscious that it felt like a very scary idea.

"You'll be okay," said Daniel.

"I hope so."

The man finished the checks and said to them,

"As soon as you feel the strain of the speedboat try to resist it at first and then run as it starts to pull you off the ground."

Both Jenny and Daniel found the idea of resisting a speed boat pulling you a rather futile idea but were ready to try anyway. In a few seconds the line of the parachute began to expand and a few seconds later the line was fully stretched. Then they felt it pulling them and they had no choice but to run, before Jenny could take two strides her feet lifted up and they were airborne. Jenny screamed as they went up and kicked her feet wildly, she grabbed Daniel's hand and as they soared higher and higher she calmed down just enough to enjoy the ride. The speedboat was roaring below them, cutting through the waves, but they could hardly hear it with the sound of the wind whistling past them. The beach became a strip on the horizon as the landscape grew up from the waves. They could see for miles all across the island. She squeezed Daniel's hand tighter and then tighter still as the speed boat slowed and they began to fall out of the air towards the sea. She panicked thinking something terrible was about to happen as their feet plunged into the sea but a second later the speedboat accelerated and they were in the air once more. It was as if they were free, flying above the troubled earth without a care in the world and all too soon it was over. A man in the speedboat indicated for them to pull the parachute control so that they would bank in towards the beach. Daniel pulled it hard and they felt the parachute move over. As they descended the warm sand appeared to come up to meet them and they both had to run as they landed so as not to be pulled over by the parachute. As soon as they were detached from the lines Jenny jumped into Daniel's arms. She still had her head in the clouds and whilst swept up in the moment she pressed her hands against his cheeks and kissed his lips. She felt him kissing her back and lifting her up and as he spun her around she let her hands fly free. It was almost like being in the sky again and as with the parasail it was only when she felt the sand beneath her feet that she knew she was on terra firma once more. She was still completely ecstatic when she saw that Daniel was looking at her with a note of concern.

"Are you all right?" he asked.

A drop of blood ran down and over her lip. Daniel dug in his pocket and handed her a handkerchief. It was a strangely old fashioned gesture but one that fitted him perfectly in that moment. Delicately Jenny wiped it away.

"It must have been all the excitement and the pressure from being up there," she said. "I'm sorry about your handkerchief."

"That does not matter as long as you are okay. It was amazing wasn't it?"

"Yes, it was breath-taking, fantastic. I'm so happy we did it together."

Neither one of them could quite describe how much they had enjoyed the experience. Perhaps it was the closest they might ever come to the feeling of flying. When they returned to their little beach set up Sarah was dumbstruck,

"Was that you? Up there?"

"Yes. It was incredible," enthused Jenny.

"I can't believe you did that," said Sarah with equal parts of astonishment and concern.

"And I would do it again and again if we could. Wouldn't you Daniel?" she said kissing him again, this time on the cheek.

Phillip stirred from his slumber with all the noise.

"What's going on? What did I miss?" said Phillip and when no one answered he asked again, "What?"

His only reply was Daniel shaking his head which he shrugged off as meaning nothing important so rolled over, and slept a while longer. They remained at the beach for several more hours before catching a bus back towards Sliema. On the journey back Phillip told the others,

"We're going to get out in St. Julian's. Any of you want to join us?"

"What's in St. Julian's?" asked Sarah.

"A lot of bars and a few clubs," said Phillip.

"That could be fun," said Sarah.

"Okay then," said Matthew.

"How about you two?" Phillip asked Daniel and Jenny.

Jenny wanted to continue the day with her friends but she felt tired after what had already been a long day for her and Daniel.

"I think I'll have to pass tonight," said Jenny.

Phillip shrugged his acceptance.

"I should go back to the hotel with you then," said Sarah.

"No you go," said Jenny "I want you to have a good time."

"I don't want to leave you on your own."

"Please go. I want you to have fun. That's why we came isn't it?"

"Yes but I don't think you should go alone."

"I could go back with her" said Daniel.

"See. I'll be fine," said Jenny.

"Okay but you take care of her," Sarah told Daniel.

"I will."

When Phillip rang the bell for the bus to stop in an area known as Paceville Sarah disembarked along with Phillip, Matthew and Lisa. Jenny looked out the window and saw a predominantly resort area with bars and restaurants everywhere. People were already roaming around the streets going from place to place, bar to bar in the run up to a long night out. Jenny waved Sarah and Lisa goodbye and Daniel moved to sit next to her and took her hand. When they arrived back at the hotel the evening meal service was almost over. Daniel escorted Jenny to her room and then left so she could shower and change in the hope of catching the end of the evening dinner service. She was getting dressed when she heard a knock on the door. It was Daniel and he had brought a tray of food,

"Room service," he said.

Jenny held the door open for him and he brought the tray in.

"We could have it on the balcony," she said opening the balcony door.

They both went outside.

"I stowed away some pastries, some fruit and cake from the buffet," he said setting the tray down.

"Thank you."

"Are you sure you're okay?"

"A little sleepy that's all. This and the fresh air should help," she said taking a bite from one of the pastries and sitting down.

The cooler night air was refreshing but it made her shiver. Jenny looked across the bay at Valletta. The illuminations from the city danced on the water hypnotically. She closed her eyes for a long moment and then opened them again to see the Carmelite Church's dome dominating the skyline just like St Paul's in London. It reminded her of home. She breathed in deeply as Daniel wrapped a blanket around her.

"Sorry. I was thinking of home."

"You don't have to be sorry," he said pulling up a chair next to her. "Are you warm enough?"

She leaned against him,

"Yes," she said feeling the warmth of his body next to hers, "it is strange isn't it?"

"What is?"

"How somewhere so far away, somewhere you've never been before, can seem like home."

She felt her mind drifting, her body was craving sleep but at that moment reality seemed more like a dream.

"I wish..." Jenny started and stopped.

"What?"

There was a long pause as she considered what she was about to say but she was too afraid that speaking the words out loud would change everything. That reality was not a dream but a terrible nightmare.

"What is it?" Daniel pressed her.

Jenny did not answer. She looked at the light on the fortress walls, the illuminated church spires, the lamps and window lights and they all fused together creating a haze in the night sky, which she imagined as the memories of the city drifting up and into the oblivion of space. It frightened her and she was afraid that all of her memories would be lost in the same void and in that instant she could not bear to be alone.

"Stay with me," she whispered.

## CHAPTER FIVE

At first all Daniel could hear were muffled sounds which gradually became more distinctive. A door closed, light footsteps, something being placed on a table. Then he caught the slightest scent of perfume and it stirred him from his sleep and compelled him to open his eyes. Daniel sat up slowly on the settee where he had spent the night and tried to roll the crick out of his neck. He still felt the morning fog in his mind.

"Good morning," said Jenny as she handed him a cup of tea.

"Morning," he replied.

She kissed him softly and tenderly on his forehead.

"Thank you," she said, "for staying."

Daniel was glad and the uncertainty of whether he had done the right thing or not vanished.

"How are you feeling today?" he asked.

"Rested and ready to go."

"I wonder if Phillip did anything crazy last night."

Jenny looked at him.

"Is it okay that you came back with me?"

Daniel stood and went over to hug her.

"More than okay."

"Even though you slept on the couch?"

"Even then," he said not wanting to let go of her.

"Maybe I could make it up to y-"

The phone rang and startled them both. Jenny answered it,

"Oh, okay. I'll be right down."

"Who was that?"

"Reception. There's a parcel."

Daniel was as intrigued as Jenny and so they both went down to reception where the receptionist handed Jenny quite a large box with a pretty bow on top of it and a card. Jenny read the card out loud,

"A memento of your time in Malta, signed Rocco."

Jenny opened the box and inside was the vase she had made at the craft village.

"That's so sweet. You have to thank your uncle for me."

Then the receptionist handed Daniel a second and much smaller box. He opened it and saw his own pottery creation. Jenny laughed as Daniel read the note his uncle had left him.

"What did he say?" asked Jenny.

Before Daniel answered Matthew came over from the lift looking rather tired.

"Reception just called about a parcel?"

Daniel showed Matthew his sad little pot.

"Oh my," then he saw Jenny's, "that's really nice."

"Thank you," said Jenny.

"You look a little the worse for wear," said Daniel.

Matthew groaned and said,

"You were right to bail out."

"Why?" asked Daniel.

"I'll tell you over coffee, a lot of coffee, and maybe some breakfast."

The three of them walked to the restaurant as Matthew resumed his story.

"Phillip took us round quite a few pubs and then to a nightclub."

"That doesn't seem too bad," said Daniel.

"No that part was fine, though I think we all drank too much. It was the journey back when Phillip insisted it was only a short walk and we made the mistake of following him. I swear he took us everywhere but in the right direction and we nearly missed every cab along the way. If we hadn't found that last taxi we'd still be lost now."

"I'm afraid Phillip has never had the best sense of direction."

"That is for sure," said Matthew. "Anyway I don't know what you had planned for today but I think you can count Phillip out until this afternoon at the earliest."

Daniel looked at Jenny, he had only been thinking of her, and he felt a little ashamed for being so selfish. He thought about the morning he and Jenny had spent in the capital.

"Maybe we should all go into Valletta," suggested Daniel.

"That sounds good," said Jenny.

"Sounds good," said Matthew.

"Why don't I go and wake the girls and get them down here for breakfast." said Jenny.

"We'll meet you in there," said Daniel.

Jenny turned round and went to fetch her friends and then after a long breakfast the five of them met outside the hotel and walked to the nearest bus stop. When the bus arrived it looked full and by the time they boarded there weren't enough seats for them all.

"There's one at the back," said Lisa.

"You take it," said Sarah to Jenny.

"I can stand."

"How long does it take?" asked Sarah.

"About forty minutes," replied Daniel.

"You should sit down," said Sarah to Jenny once more.

"I'm standing. One of you sit down," said Jenny

The last people boarded the bus and it pulled away. Lisa almost fell into the seat. A few stops later another seat opened up. Daniel pointed it out to Jenny but she remained resolute and continued standing.

"You did pay for the ticket," said Daniel, "you should at least have a seat."

"I'm perfectly fine here."

"Sit down," said Sarah.

"You first," replied Jenny.

Sarah relented and took the empty seat and tried to make enough room for Jenny to squeeze on too but couldn't. The bus continued on its route and it was another ten minutes before another seat opened up at the back.

"Now will you sit down," said Jenny to Daniel.

He refused to budge.

"Stop being so gallant," Jenny said and pushed him backwards onto the seat.

The bus lurched away violently and Jenny lost her footing. She fell on top of Daniel.

"How about now?" asked Daniel.

"Very well," Jenny said and sat on his lap.

"That wasn't quite what I had in mind."

"No?"

"No."

"I can stand up again if you'd prefer?"

"No you don't have to. I don't mind."

Daniel tried to remain as chivalrous as possible but he couldn't help think how good she felt to him. He tried to purge any kind of desire from his mind and to think of anything that might distract him. First he looked around the bus, it was still quite full. Matthew was there, still standing, along with several other people. At the next stops more people boarded and it became completely overcrowded. Even those standing were pressing up against each other and the bus was getting warmer, he thought. He could feel Jenny's body pressed up against his, could smell her perfume, his arm was wrapped around her, holding her and he really wanted to kiss her again. His methods for distracting himself were failing and so it came as a mixed blessing when they arrived at the terminus.

Everyone got off the bus and they all made their way into Valletta. Daniel played the tour guide for them all, taking them through the high street, and to several of the places he had mentioned to Jenny on their first visit. Time seemed to go by quickly and a little after midday everyone was hungry and decided that it was lunchtime. They went to a piazza, which Daniel called Queen's Square, for lunch. The square was enclosed by buildings on three sides. On two sides there were restaurants outside of which were lines of tables and parasols. A line through the middle was kept clear and at the end was a statue of Queen Victoria. They picked a restaurant and stopped for lunch whilst around them the siesta overtook the city. By the time they resumed their tour it was as if the whole city had gone silent. A strange experience to those not used to it, seeing a city sleep in the middle of the day, but by mid-afternoon the siesta was coming to an end and slowly but surely the residents began to open the shops and other services once more. It was also the time for Daniel to visit his grandparents. He looked at his little group and did not quite know what to do.

"What's the matter?" asked Jenny.

"I said I'd go and see my grandparents in a few minutes."

"That's okay. You should go."

"What about you?" he said to Jenny.

"We'll be fine."

"Are you sure you don't mind?"

"Of course not. They're your family."

"I can stay with them and we can meet you at the opera house," said Matthew.

"I'll be a couple of hours."

"Go already," said Jenny.

"What will you do?"

"Oh I don't know," said Jenny looking around at all the shops opening up.

"In that case I'll leave you to it," said Daniel making a quick exit. "Sorry Matthew."

As he was walking away he looked behind him and saw Matthew, who was wishing he hadn't said he would stay, as the girls took him along into the first shop. Daniel navigated around a couple of streets and made his way to his grandparents. He entered the building through the main entrance and climbed up to the top floor. Knocking on the old wooden door his grandmother opened it. She invited him in with a hug and kissed him on both cheeks.

"Go through, go through. I just made tea."

Daniel went through to the living room where he saw his grandfather and Phillip both enjoying a cup of tea.

"Ah, there you are my boy," said William. "Come sit down. Vi? Vi get Daniel some tea."

Daniel sat down and his grandmother poured him a cup of tea, her hands shook a little as she passed it to him and the tea spilt onto the saucer. Daniel lifted the cup and drank from the saucer.

"That's a good idea," said William, "don't waste a drop."

"Did you know that building near the hotel was an abandoned barracks?" Phillip asked Daniel.

"No."

"Oh, you don't know?" said William. "The British built them and a school and a church, St. Luke's I think. Of course they were all abandoned when they left."

"They look rather derelict," said Daniel.

"Yes. We move on, build new things and forget the past," said William.

Daniel looked at his grandfather. He always seemed so positive managing to find the best even in the worst situations, including two World Wars that were beyond Daniel's comprehension.

"Maybe they'll repair them," said Phillip.

"In time, perhaps, we'll see," said William. "But what about now? You are both enjoying the sun? The food?"

"Of course," answered Daniel and Phillip.

"That's good," said William,

"You are both well?" asked Violet.

"Yes," said Daniel.

"Sure," said Phillip.

"Good, good," said William. "You have enough tea?"

Before either of them could answer their grandmother was filling their cups again.

"How are your friends?" asked William.

"Matthew's good," said Phillip.

Daniel instantly thought about Jenny and wondered what she was doing right at that moment.

"He's doing a little shopping," said Daniel.

"Here?" asked Violet.

"Yes, in Valletta."

"Ah, we have so many shops now. I don't get to them as much as I used to. I used to like the shops in England, like your Marks and Spencer. We have that here too."

"We don't have as many small shops these days," said Phillip.

"But you still have the fish and chip shop?" asked William.

"Of course," said Phillip.

"I like the chips when they're cold, you know?"

Daniel smiled with the half-forgotten memory.

"So I took a siesta earlier and now we take a walk," said William.

Both Daniel and Phillip finished their tea, took the cups and saucers to the kitchen, said goodbye to their grandmother and followed William out into the streets of Valletta. William seldom took them to the places most tourists would see instead he showed them the places he had known all his life. He delighted in telling them the history behind not only the buildings but the people that had lived in them over the decades. They walked out to the edges of the city and followed the footpath around until they came to a good vantage point looking out across the bay towards Sliema. They stopped to take in the view and William pointed to a spot in the distance.

"Your gran and I first lived there, when we were married."

"I didn't know that," said Daniel.

"Oh she was the prettiest girl. From there, we moved to another place when we had your uncles, and here after we had your father," said William pointing places out in the distance.

Daniel did not know what to say, he felt as if he lacked any of the life experiences to be able to really talk to his grandfather. How could anything he had seen or done compare to such a long life, filled with family and friends and events that had shaped history? He wondered if his brother felt the same and what both their lives might be like when they were the same age as William. Could he spend the next seventy years with one person, build a family and a home together? As Daniel tried to imagine it, he came back to the same image over and over again. He saw Jenny, he saw them getting married, their first child, their first home, how they grew old together and it was all he wanted.

"You're far away," said William.

Daniel took a breath but did not know what to say. William took a step forwards and took his arm.

"What is troubling you?" asked William.

Daniel looked over at Phillip who was still admiring the view. William took Phillip's arm too.

"You are both troubled I think," said William. "Let's walk a little more."

They both walked with William. Daniel was not sure how he could say anything when his relationship had really only just begun. Phillip was equally quiet.

"Everything seems difficult?" asked William.

"Maybe. I guess I thought things would follow an order," said Daniel.

"Such as?" asked William.

"You go to school, university, then get a job and a family."

"You are both still young. Phillip is starting his job soon."

"Yeah," said Phillip.

"And sometimes it takes time for everything else to happen."

"What if it doesn't happen though?" asked Daniel.

"It nearly didn't happen with your gran and I."

"It didn't?" asked Phillip.

"She made me work for her hand but I kept going until she said yes."

"And after that?" asked Daniel.

"We had a family, and now we have you boys but it was never simple. At times we didn't have much but we made do. We made the best of things and that is often all you can do."

Daniel did not know what Phillip wanted but he knew he had to make the best of things with Jenny. He told himself that he had to make every moment count.

"You both have time for many more adventures yes?" William asked looking from Daniel to Phillip.

"I guess so," said Phillip.

"You will. It is a blessing to be young to have your lives ahead of you. So now I return to your gran and you will find your friends and enjoy your time together. Find new things to come back and tell us about."

"We will," said Daniel wondering if there was some hidden meaning behind what William was saying but mostly he thought he was telling them both to live.

William took them back to the main high street where he prepared to let them go,

"You know your gran and I think of you both a lot."

"We think of you too," said Daniel.

They shook hands and watched as William walked back home. Phillip moved a little closer to Daniel.

"Should we find Matthew?"

"Yes. I said we'd meet up again at the opera house, about half an hour from now."

"Is Lisa with him?"

"The girls went shopping too."

"That's probably expensive."

"Probably."

They both lingered awkwardly.

"Let's head over to the opera house," said Daniel.

Phillip agreed and they made their way through the city centre and to the ruined opera house. The others were not there yet so they found a good spot to sit and watch amid the ruins.

"No book today?" asked Daniel.

"It's drying out."

Daniel decided it was better not to ask.

"You and Lisa seem to be getting on well."

"Yeah I guess so."

"Do you think you'll see her when we get back?"

"Maybe."

Phillip looked bored and Daniel did not really know what to say. His brother might have been a born talker but it seemed over the years they had run out of things to say to each other. Phillip checked his watch again and then lay down on one of the large stones. Daniel continued people watching, hoping to see Jenny in the crowd. They waited a further twenty minutes before Daniel saw them. They had loaded Matthew up with several bags and he looked like he had endured a marathon. As they began the return journey to Sliema the girls told Daniel and Phillip that they had a plan for the night and they would have to dress smartly.

Once back at the hotel the boys went to their room to change whilst the girls did the same and in the early evening Daniel returned to Jenny's room and knocked on the door. He waited and continued waiting. He thought about knocking again but he heard someone approaching the door. When she opened the door Daniel gazed at her in amazement. Her hair was up with two long curls dropping down and outlining the sides of her face. She wore a little eye shadow that drew him to gaze into her hazel eyes and then down to her lips coated in a seductive shade of red. Her dress flowed around the contours of her body as if she had been draped by a curtain of night, with the stars shining out of the material.

"You look handsome," said Jenny.

Daniel hardly registered what she had said as he was still staring at her. Jenny pulled the straps of the dress up a little on her shoulders. He didn't mean to stare at her chest but he did and so he tried to look down only to see the slit in her dress which extended up to her thigh and that made his heart skip another beat.

"You are beautiful," said Daniel.

"Thank you."

Daniel extended his arm and Jenny linked her arm with his. Together they took the lift down to the ground floor and stepped out. The reception was full of people, new holidaymakers checking in, those checking out, and people in-between places making Daniel and Jenny weave between them to join the others so they could make their way to the casino. Outside the hotel two taxis were waiting for them. The drivers made a show of opening the doors for the ladies. Sarah shared the first taxi with Lisa and Phillip whilst Matthew took the front seat in the taxi with Daniel and Jenny. It was a short trip to the casino but on route Daniel felt Jenny's hand on his leg, her touch filled him with confidence and her presence made him feel like the luckiest person alive. They followed the other taxi out of the inner streets of Sliema and into St. Julian's where they drove along the coast road until the lights of the casino grew ever brighter and closer until they arrived.

They went through the main entrance of the casino, past the doormen, and through into the lobby. The lobby was lavishly detailed with oak panels adorning the lower half of the walls and the rest of the wall was an off white. The wooden floor was highly polished with a variety of plush seating scattered around. From the lobby two massive wooden doors led to the spiralling staircases which fanned out onto the casino floor where there were rows of bandit machines, wheels of fortune, card tables, craps tables, roulette wheels and a long wide bar at the far end. They all took their time deciding on what appealed to them. Phillip and Lisa headed towards the bar, whilst Matthew and Sarah stayed with Daniel and Jenny. The four of them made their way through the casino to the exchange booths where they bought some tokens. At first they only felt brave enough to try out the one arm bandits whilst they looked around and tried to figure out the games.

"Do you know how to play any of the games?" asked Jenny.

"Not really," said Daniel.

"How about the wheel of fortune?" asked Sarah.

"Do you want to try?" Jenny asked Daniel.

"Okay, what about you Matthew?"

"I'm getting to grips with this machine. I'll catch up with you."

The three of them moved over to the wheel whilst Matthew stayed at the bandit machine figuring it out. At the wheel they would spin it and felt as if it was going to be close but then it missed often by the narrowest amount possible and so they moved on to look at the craps tables.

"How do you play?" asked Sarah.

"I don't know," said Jenny.

They both looked at Daniel who said,

"I have no idea."

A cheer went up from the table but Daniel was none the wiser.

"How about blackjack?" he asked.

"Okay," they both agreed.

Daniel thought blackjack was a lot simpler.

"How do you play?" asked Jenny.

"You have to get twenty one, but no more or you go bust."

They stayed at the blackjack table for several hands but Daniel saw that Jenny was not fully engaged by the game.

"How about a drink?" asked Daniel.

"That would be good," said Jenny.

"I'm going to play a little more," said Sarah.

Daniel looked around and saw that there was a viewing gallery on the floor above. They went to it, ordered a couple of drinks, sat down and watched the games going on below them. They saw Phillip and Lisa in the far corner beginning to experiment with a few fruit machines. Matthew was still at his one armed bandit and Sarah was quite engrossed with the game of blackjack.

"So is it a good surprise?" asked Jenny.

"It is. I've never been to a casino before. It's kind of crazy."

"Yes. So many people."

"I wonder how many fortunes have been made and lost in places like this."

"Too many," said Jenny.

"I guess it's okay if you only risk what you can afford."

His words seemed to resonate with her and he was asking himself the same question. How much could he afford to risk with her?

"That depends on if you're willing to gamble in the first place," said Jenny.

"I am. Are you?"

"I don't know. What if the game is rigged?"

"You have to play before you can find that out."

"Even if you stand to lose everything?"

"I don't know. I've never had much to lose," until now he thought.

Daniel could see that Jenny wanted to say something else but it was if she did not know how or perhaps she did not feel it was the right time or place. It made him all the more curious about her.

"Do you want to try roulette?" asked Daniel.

"Why not."

They found a quieter roulette table and watched for a while until they felt confident enough to place a bet. At first they both bet on black or red, odd or even, so one or other of them inevitably won. Then they decided to be a little more adventurous and bet on a block of numbers.

"What date is your birthday?" asked Jenny.

"The thirtieth."

Jenny placed her bet on thirty and three adjoining numbers. The wheel was spun and the ball rolled and rolled. Gradually the wheel slowed and the ball clattered over the numbers and landed on thirty-one. It was one of Jenny's block and she jumped with joy and let out a little scream of excitement.

"Beginners luck," she said hugging Daniel.

"Do you want to try again?" asked the croupier.

"No, I could only ever be that lucky once," said Jenny.

"And you sir?"

"I'm done too."

They left the table and went back over to Matthew.

"We're going to slip away," said Daniel.

"Oh okay," said Matthew realising how much time he spent at the same machine. "I guess I might as well stay until it eats all my tokens."

"Would you tell the others we left?" asked Jenny.

"Yes, of course."

Matthew appeared to be about to say something else but he changed his mind and simply wished them goodnight. Outside the casino there was an old man with a horse and karozzin carriage. The horse was jet black, standing at over sixteen hands and was finishing a feedbag. Jenny really wanted to make a fuss of the horse but Daniel still seemed uncertain.

"You can pet her," said the old man.

Daniel waited patiently as Jenny became friends with the horse. He looked at the small two seat carriage, the dark wood appeared black in the night, the fabric roof almost floated on the small supports, wrapped with tied back curtains.

"She likes you," the old man said to Jenny as he removed the feedbag. "Where are you heading?"

"Back to Sliema," said Daniel.

"I can take you part way if you like. We're finishing for the night."

The old man lit the lanterns on the carriage and checked the harness.

"How long have you had her?" asked Jenny.

"Fifteen years now. We'll both soon be retired. We can't keep up with the younger ones. Don't really want to. Out all day in the blazing heat. It's too hot for horse and man."

"Well we were heading to Tigné Point," said Daniel.

"We'll get you half way there if you like."

"Would you like a short ride?" Daniel asked Jenny.

It was a redundant question as Jenny walked over to the carriage and climbed on. Once Daniel was seated next to her the old man gently jingled the reins and the jet black horse pulled them onwards. As the horse and carriage followed the coast he wondered what Jenny was thinking at that moment, with the cooler night air around them and the sound of the waves washing against the rocky shore. He gazed upon her. She was smiling and the soft lights of the street lamps gave her skin a warm complexion. Jenny seemed to sense him looking at her and she turned to face him. Daniel searched his mind for what he wanted to say.

"I've had such an amazing time with you. I wonder if…" he said.

"If what?" she said encouraging him to continue.

"If you wanted to take another risk, a gamble on me. On us?"

Jenny's smile warmed him and she took his hand.

"I'd love to but..."

He felt himself shudder waiting for whatever might possibly follow.

"What if…" her speech trailed off and she took a long deep pause, "what if there's something you don't know about me."

"There's a lot we don't know about each other."

"Yes, of course there is but I don't want you to get hurt."

"I don't want you to get hurt either. It's a chance, but one I want to take."

"I want to take that chance too but-"

Daniel kissed her. As they pulled away they could hear each other breathing.

"I've never felt this way before," said Jenny.

Her lips gently pressed against his as she kissed him back.

"I'm a little frightened," she said.

Her hair blew in front of her face.

"Why?" asked Daniel brushing her hair away.

"Because I'm falling in love with you."

Her lower lip trembled slightly forcing her to softly bite it to stop it shaking. Daniel wanted to tell her that he felt the same way but as she looked up into his eyes words failed them both. His heart was still racing. Everything about her was perfect to him. He tried to take in every detail at that moment so he would always remember it when he realised they were stopped. How long had they been sat there he asked himself? They both felt a little embarrassed as they realised the old man was watching them, his hand on his heart.

"Such young love," he said.

"I'm sorry," said Daniel, "I didn't realise where we

were."

"No, no, you both stay. Now we can continue all the way."

## Chapter Six

They returned to Jenny's room where she asked Daniel to unfasten the back of her dress. He fumbled slightly but released the clasps. With them undone she went into the bathroom to change. Jenny had never expected that anything like this could happen to her. Already she felt that her life was forever changed and she was happy for now she knew what it was like to fall madly in love. As Jenny peeled off her dress she caught a glimpse of herself in the mirror and she felt very nervous and very conscious of her own body. All at once she wanted to feel sexy but she was scared to let Daniel see her. She tried to rationalise that he had already seen her in a bathing costume but this felt very different. It was different. Jenny could not overcome her inhibitions and so put on her nightgown afraid that even that showed too much.

When she came out she saw that Daniel was sitting on the sofa. Still filled with doubts and desires she called to him,

"Daniel."

Her voice sounded different in her own head but he came to her and leaned heavily against the door frame. His eyes seemed to be burning, and she desperately wanted him to touch her but still there was a fear deep within her and it was growing with every passing second. Jenny sat on the edge of the bed and saw him watching her. She felt like a young girl with her first crush and she wondered if he was feeling the same way. He did seem nervous and uncertain she thought. It was not like a film where the man would confidently sweep her up in his arms and take her to bed. Her mind kept racing but she was unable to make any decisions.

"This is crazy," said Daniel.

"I know."

"I feel like I've known you my whole life. It's such a trite thing to say but it's true."

"I feel the same way."

"That it's trite and clichéd?"

"No. That we've known each other longer than we have even if it is a cliché."

"Does it matter how long it has been?" asked Daniel.

"I'm not sure. It doesn't seem to matter to some people."

"Does it matter to you?"

"A little, I think."

"Me too and I hate that it does because all I can think of right now is coming in there and kissing you."

Jenny gave him a nervous smile as she could see him pressing half his body against the door frame, itching to come over to her.

"What should we do?" he asked her.

Jenny stood up and went over to Daniel. She kissed him and said,

"Can you wait, a little longer?"

"Yes," he said.

"I still want you to stay," said Jenny.

"I will."

Jenny watched as Daniel lay down on the settee. She returned to her own bed and that night she watched as he fell asleep. Soon afterwards she was seduced into her own dreams.

The next morning Jenny woke Daniel early.

"Can we go somewhere, just the two of us?" she asked.

Only half awake he was a little groggy and it took him a few seconds to figure out what she was saying but when it clicked he agreed. They left a message at reception for the others simply saying that they had headed out exploring and then they caught a bus to the end of the line, Ċirkewwa Ferry Terminal. Jenny looked out of the bus window as they passed through St. Julian's and she thought of their night at the casino and the carriage ride. She glanced over at Daniel, still in the suit from that night having only discarded his tie. At the end of the ride she saw the terminal which appeared to claw out into the sea and there was a Gozo Channel Line ferry filling up with people and cars and coaches. In the distance she could see two islands, one was Comino, and the other Gozo. She followed Daniel as they walked onto the ferry; through a hatch, up a ladder to the upper deck and then to the bow where they sat and watched the sea splash against the ferry as it began the crossing. During the half hour crossing Jenny looked behind them at Malta and then ahead at Gozo where she could make out rocky cliffs and green fields. The ferry docked at Mġarr on the island of Gozo where everyone disembarked. The harbour was busy with the ferry's arrival creating a hub of activity. Jenny kept hold of Daniel's hand to prevent getting turned around with all the people swiftly heading off to their own destinations but she had no idea where they were going. She followed Daniel around the harbour a little way until they came to the bus stop. They got on the waiting bus and as soon as it pulled away it was like going back in time. The hustle and bustle that they had become accustomed to on Malta and at the harbour vanished and was replaced by a far more serene atmosphere. They travelled through several small and picturesque villages until they arrived at Victoria, the capital of Gozo where Jenny saw the Citadel in the distance. Daniel told her that they would be coming back there as all roads led to the Citadel but for now they had to change buses, which they did and so they began to leave Victoria behind and went out to Għarb. The short journey was even more rural with little but the rocky countryside and churches in sight. When Daniel saw the village square he rang the bell and they jumped out. Jenny was intrigued by the church which had an elaborate baroque façade which could have been equally at home in Rome as it was in the small village. Jenny studied it for several minutes, walking around it and admiring the craftsmanship of the sculptures when she noticed that on the two belfries there were what appeared to be two clocks except the right one was an inscription that read, 'Ibni għozz iz-zmien'. She asked Daniel what it meant but he did not know and so Jenny scribbled it on a piece of paper hoping to ask someone later. As they continued to walk through the village they saw a group of older ladies sitting outside their front doors with what looked like spiked clubs in their laps. Daniel told her that they were making lace and when she looked closer she could see that the spikes were pins arranged in patterns and the ladies worked a dozen bobbins at a time to form the intricate designs. She watched them with fascination for several minutes before they continued on their way out of the village and into the Gozitan countryside. In the distance Jenny could see the sea and the hilly terrain broke through the land into sheer cliffs.

They began the ascent up the cliffs searching out the easiest paths they could find. When they came to a trickier spot Daniel would help Jenny and she would return the favour. Once they reached the top of the cliff they stopped to take a proper look down over the edge at the Inland Sea, a lagoon of seawater linked to the Mediterranean through a narrow arch. They watched the luzzu fishing boats bobbing in the water, their vibrant colours seemed to glow over the water's surface. From their position on top of the cliffs they looked over Gozo and the sea that enclosed it and Jenny felt as if they were truly alone on the island. Daniel took her hand and led her over towards the other side of the rocks where the life blood of the lagoon washed in. She could not see the archway beneath the layers of rock under her feet but there was a strong breeze swirling all around them coming from the sea and when the wind gusted she felt exhilarated. The wind was strong enough to push her backwards. The longer she resisted the force of the wind the more free she felt.

Jenny followed Daniel around the lagoon and they began descending from the cliffs until they were once more at sea level. They walked around the base of the cliffs out over the shore until she saw the Azure Window, a natural limestone arch standing nearly thirty metres high and jutting out into the sea, where the tide was lashing it with powerful waves that smashed against the rock.

"We were up there," said Daniel as he pointed to the cliffs above.

"This place never stops amazing me."

"I hoped you would feel that way."

"I wish we could stay."

"There never seems enough time does there?"

"No. There really isn't."

She felt a wave of sadness come over her.

"What's the matter?" he asked.

Again Jenny felt that she wanted to say more but it felt as if it were impossible. She had desperately wanted to spend some time alone with Daniel and she was afraid that she was ruining everything when all she wanted was to enjoy their time together.

"Nothing, I'm being silly," she said before replacing her sadness with a forced smile.

"How about lunch and then an ice cream?" asked Daniel.

Jenny's spirits lifted over the course of the meal and her forced smile became a real one by the time they started dessert. They left Dwejra and the Azure Window behind and headed back to Victoria where Jenny delighted in exploring the Citadel, with the baroque cathedral and the stunning tromp l'oeil, a painting that created an optical illusion to give the impression of a dome that was never built. It was mid-afternoon when they decided to take in one more stop. They took the bus from Victoria out to Qala where they were greeted by another church.

"How many churches are there?" asked Jenny.

"One for every day of the year," said Daniel.

"Very funny."

"No seriously. There's hundreds of them. I honestly think there might be one for every day of the year."

"For as small as these islands are that seems a little crazy."

"I guess Paul was a very good missionary."

Jenny looked at him with a blank expression compelling him to elaborate.

"St. Paul was shipwrecked here when he was being taken to Rome. There's a little island between Mellieha Bay and St. Paul's Bay. Well I guess the name kind of says it all."

They continued talking and walking out of Qala towards the coast.

"Do you think it is true, that he really was shipwrecked here?"

"I think so. There's a lot of stories about it and Malta converted to Christianity early considering it was a Roman colony."

"I can't believe you know all of this."

"I was brought up with it. Stories about the Second World War, the Knights of St. John, and St. Paul's shipwreck and the snake bite."

"What snake bite?"

"Well the legend is that Paul was bitten by a poisonous snake, but it had no effect on him."

"There are poisonous snakes here?"

She felt a shudder go through her as she said it.

"Oh yes, at least four types in fact. There's a Cat Snake, a Leopard Snake, an Algerian Whip Snake and the biggest of them all the Black Whip Snake."

Jenny felt her skin crawl.

"Are they dangerous?" she asked.

"Well that depends…"

She felt Daniel slide his hand over her back.

"Stop it."

Daniel laughed.

"I've never actually seen one and I don't think any of them are harmful to humans."

Jenny was not entirely reassured and she kept looking at the ground as they were walking for any sign of snakes.

After another twenty minutes they came to Hondoq ir-Rummien, a small sandy beach where the normal tranquil and clear waters were becoming more tempestuous. They continued from the beach around the coast a little more heading back in the direction of Mġarr until they reached a high spot where they stopped and took a seat on a suitably rocky outcrop to look out over the sea. As Jenny sat there watching the waves grow larger and larger the last lingering thoughts of creepy crawlies vanished from her mind.

"Is it far to the ferry?" she asked.

"Half an hour's walk along the coast."

She leaned against Daniel and rested her head on his shoulder.

"Is that Malta?" she asked looking out past the smaller island of Comino.

"Yes."

"Do we have to go back?"

"Soon."

"I really don't want it to end."

"It doesn't have to does it?"

"I wish it didn't but there is something I have to tell you but I don't want to."

No matter how she tried to put the words together she failed every time. It was as if saying it would make it too real, even though it was already true. Jenny watched the sea. How it eroded the rock until there was nothing left but sediment. That sediment though could be reborn into a new kind of stone. It was nature's way. To destroy and to create. She looked at Daniel who was waiting for her to say something more, she had to try, she owed him that much because she loved him.

"We both have lave lives back home," she said.

Daniel looked into her eyes and she felt her will to continue evaporating rapidly.

"And things aren't always simple and well the-"

Daniel kissed her. She tried to resist,

"Well the thing is-"

He continued kissing her and she gave in. She knew it was wrong but it was all she wanted. It was all some part of her had ever wanted. To be loved.

They remained looking out over the sea until they knew they had to return to the ferry and so continued the last leg of the journey along the coast back to Mġarr where the ferry was waiting. They bought their tickets and went aboard as a few drops of rain began to fall. The rain took them by surprise and Jenny imagined they were the tears of the island because they had to part. It seemed everyone knew there was a storm coming and they crowded into the sheltered parts of the ferry as the rain began to pour. The crossing was rough, the ship pressed through the waves that rocked the vessel. Jenny watched as Daniel became more and more uncomfortable and he excused himself to go outside despite the weather. He stood on the deck holding onto the rail. She followed him,

"Are you okay?"

"I'm not great with boats and I really don't want to

embarrass myself in front of you."

"I don't care if you embarrass yourself," she said putting her hand on his back.

Together they waited out the journey outside in the rain with only partial cover from the overhead deck. Jenny held onto Daniel the whole time, resting her head on his back, and he never embarrassed himself. By the time they docked at Ċirkewwa in Malta the rain had slowed to a drizzle. They found the bus to Sliema and got on board glad to be off the ferry and out of the rain. Jenny took a towel from her beach bag and attempted to dry them both off a little but Daniel was completely soaked from the rain and the sea spray. The bus was warm and after a short while Jenny felt her eye lids closing and she slumped against Daniel. She remembered he put his arm around her and that he had stroked her hair and then there was nothing.

An hour later she heard Daniel,

"We're back. Time to wake up."

She sat upright and looked out of the window into the night and didn't quite realise where she was.

"Where are we?"

"In Sliema. It's nearly our stop."

"Oh. I was asleep."

"I know."

"We're back?"

"Yes."

Daniel reached up and rang the bell for the bus to stop. Jenny still felt disorientated and the walk from the bus to the hotel all seemed to take place in brief flashes. A flash of the Sliema promenade, the exterior of the hotel, the reception, an out of order sign on the lifts, the stairs, her arm around Daniel as he picked her up and carried her to her room, him setting her down on the bed, he said something to her, kissed her and then she was asleep but her sleep was far from restful. Her mind filled with the image of Daniel and herself standing together on the cliff tops of Gozo. They stood there all alone with the wind blowing gently all round them as she fell into his embrace. The wind began to blow wildly all around them, blowing her hair over him. She felt herself crying. Daniel tried to sooth her but all of his words were carried away by the wind. She could not hear him, but she could feel his presence as the wind became deafening. Her tears began to blur his image, he became distant but she could still feel him holding her arms. Jenny did not struggle and felt his energy pouring out and with it she felt his love for her. Daniel half pulled her towards him and their bodies pressed together. Her tears cleared and as she looked into his loving eyes their lips touched. Her soft lips caressed over his and then their two beings became intertwined as their very souls merged together. Every sense was tingling with his presence as the wind howled around them fanning their burning passion. She felt that nothing would break that moment, that it would last forever as if set in stone but even stone erodes. Jenny's hands fell away from Daniel's face and she leaned back from him, forcing him to let her go. She looked down at her own hands as they shrivelled becoming brittle and old. Jenny looked back at Daniel, but for all his strength, all his love he could do nothing. In the reflection of his eyes she saw her face age rapidly, wrinkles gathered, her firm body began to sag, her bones ached under her own weight. Jenny tried to scream out loud but the wind took hold of the sound and it was lost. Daniel stretched forth his hand, he was still young and beautiful. Jenny stepped backwards only to find the cliff behind her had crumbled away with the decay that had seized her. Jenny fell, she kept falling even as Daniel reached out to her and she knew that she would never feel his presence or touch again. She plummeted into the sea, its salty water pulled her into its depths, obliterating any sign of Daniel. It pulled her further down, onto the cold sea bed, where sediments began to accumulate around her and on top of her until she felt herself become stone and everything was cold and dark.

## Chapter Seven

Daniel was awoken in the middle of the night by a cool breeze from the open balcony door. He got up from his makeshift bed and went out to the balcony where he saw Jenny staring at the sea. He thought he saw the traces of tears on her cheeks in the moonlight.

"What's the matter?" he asked.

She looked at him with tears still in her eyes.

"You can tell me," said Daniel.

"I'm being silly, it was nothing but a bad dream."

"A nightmare?"

"I'm not sure."

"Is there anything I can do? If it's me then..."

"No, it's not you. I love you."

"You do? You really do?"

"Yes. I really do. More than I can tell you."

He did not know what to say. No one had ever said they loved him before, not like that.

"You know I feel the same?"

"I think so," she said but her voice was soft and trembling. "I've never been this happy."

"Then why are you crying?"

"Because I'm happy."

"That makes no sense."

"Maybe not," she said standing up and taking his hand. "All I want is for you to stay with me."

"I will," said Daniel moving towards the settee.

Jenny took his arm and pulled him back towards the bedroom.

"Not out there. Stay with me here," she said pushing him down onto the bed. "I want to fall asleep in your arms."

He wrapped his arms around her and she pushed back against him to be as close as she could and they slept together till morning.

When Daniel woke Jenny was by his side still sleeping. He watched her chest rise and fall as she breathed and he looked at her face. She was peaceful, no more bad dreams like last night, he thought to himself. What had upset her so much he wondered? He had thought about pushing the matter further at the time but she said that she was happy. Had he imagined her sadness he asked himself? He knew that was not the case and as he looked at her the last thing he wanted to do was bring back bad memories or worse to drive her away. All Daniel wanted was for them to spend every second together. Jenny stirred and he watched her as she began to wake. Her eyes opened, squinted with the light until they adjusted and she looked straight at him and smiled. How many times had she smiled at him? He did not know but every time it made him feel like it was the best day of his life.

"Good morning," she said.

"You are stunning."

Jenny brushed at her tangled hair.

"Really?" she asked.

"If I could wake up every morning and see you just like this then mornings would be worth waking up for."

"Charmer."

She propped herself up on a couple of pillows so she could look at him clearly.

"You are…" she said thinking.

"Go on," said Daniel fishing.

"You are still here."

"Yes I am. Is that okay?"

"Definitely but…"

"But what?"

"You need some more clothes."

Daniel realised that all he had was the suit from two days ago.

"I think I'd better change," he said.

"Yes," Jenny looked at the clock, "and quickly if you want to make breakfast."

Daniel looked at the clock too and saw that they did not have long until the morning's final service. He kissed her on the cheek.

"I'll meet you down there in ten minutes."

"Okay."

He sat back down on the bed and kissed her on the lips.

"You have to go," she said still kissing him.

"I'm going," he said kissing her again.

"Go."

Jenny pushed him away gently but he lingered not wanting to leave her.

"Go," she said again.

Daniel hesitated all the way to and out of her room. As soon as the door was closed he imagined what Jenny was doing at that moment on the other side of the door. He walked to the lift glancing back at her room most of the way. The elevator was still out of commission and so he had to take the stairs up to the top floor and on entering his own room he found it empty. He guessed that Phillip and Matthew might have gone out or still be at breakfast and so he changed as quickly as possible before hurriedly heading down to the restaurant, not because he was hungry but because he wanted to see Jenny as soon as possible.

In the restaurant Daniel saw Phillip, Matthew, Sarah and Lisa all having breakfast together and so he fetched his own and went over to join them. As he approached he began to try and think how he was going to explain his absence.

"Morning," said Matthew.

"Good morning," replied Daniel, "and morning," he said to everyone else at the table.

"Morning," they all answered.

He noticed that Sarah was staring at him but tried to pretend he did not notice as he sat down and waited for the awkward questions and more importantly for Jenny.

"So…" began Phillip.

The thought of his brother interrogating him made him feel a little nauseous and indignant and so he braced himself. Phillip continued,

"I thought we might head to a different beach today."

"Okay, sure, that sounds good," said Daniel.

Then he noticed that Sarah wasn't the only one staring at him, Matthew was too.

"Which beach were you thinking?" asked Daniel.

Phillip gave Daniel a mischievous look accompanied by an equally troublesome grin.

"Ġnejna Bay."

"Oh okay," said Daniel glad not to be answering any awkward questions.

"It sounds a little more private than Mellieha," said Sarah innocently.

"Yeah sure," said Daniel still glad not to be the focus of attention but his instincts were telling him to listen more carefully. "Did you say Ġnejna Bay?" he asked Phillip.

"Yes."

"Now hold on a second," said Daniel, "you do know that-"

"Yep," said Phillip, his grin from ear to ear.

"Know what?" asked Matthew.

"Did Phillip tell you that it's a…" said Daniel.

"A what?" asked Sarah.

"Well it's just that it, Ġnejna Bay, is an unofficial, and frowned upon…"

"What?" demanded Matthew.

"A nudist beach."

"A what?" said Sarah indignantly. "Did you know that?" she asked Lisa.

Lisa shrugged nonchalantly.

"Well I'm not bloody well going to a nudist beach," said Matthew.

"It was worth a try," said Phillip feigning innocence.

There was a general jeering and tutting towards Phillip when Jenny arrived.

"What's going on?" she asked.

"My brother is trying to get us all to go a nudist beach," said Daniel.

Jenny looked at Sarah who was still rather upset and at Lisa who was completely unconcerned.

"You don't have to go nude," said Phillip.

"I'd rather not go nude or see anyone else nude for that matter," said Sarah.

"It is technically illegal," said Daniel.

"What?" said Matthew glaring at Phillip.

"Okay, okay. We'll go to a different beach. I don't see what all the fuss is for."

"There are two more beaches in the same area, and they are all family friendly," said Daniel.

"Fine," said Phillip glad to no longer be the centre of unwanted attention.

"That sounds better," said Sarah. "How was your day?" she asked Jenny.

"Oh it was good."

"Oh yeah," said Phillip, "Daniel took you on some architectural tour or something like that?"

"That's right isn't it Daniel?" said Matthew.

Daniel realised that Matthew had covered for him with his brother and he was particularly glad of it.

"Yes, we saw quite a lot. Thank you," said Daniel emphasising the last part towards Matthew.

"That's good," said Matthew.

"A lazy and relaxing day sounds good for today though," said Jenny.

It seemed that she understood the subtext happening between Daniel and his brother and for that he felt himself fall in love with her a little bit more.

During the rest of breakfast Daniel and Jenny tried not to look at each other too much but it was difficult. They had to settle for secretly holding hands under the table whenever they could or gentle knee taps. When everyone was finished they left the hotel and caught a bus from Sliema to near Għajn Tuffieħa and the beaches. At first they went to Golden Bay but it was already quite busy and so they took a short walk down to Għajn Tuffieħa Bay where they strolled up the hill and then down two hundred steps on the other side to reach the quieter red beach. There was still a good number of people there but they had plenty of space to themselves where they could set up their new beach encampment. Daniel looked at the little bay, enclosed like a horseshoe by hills, rocky outcrops and cliffs with an ancient watch tower sat atop the plateau. The water was still a little choppy from last night's storm but people were swimming in the shallows and enjoying the tranquillity of nature. The sun's rays encouraged them all to relax and bask on the beach for much of the morning. Daniel stayed by Jenny's side, keeping their affections for each other discrete but unable to quite contain them. They lay on the beach looking at the water, the shoreline, the sky and then at each other and every time she looked at him she would smile. Daniel believed that she must have known the power she held over him for he found her utterly enchanting. He still could not believe how his perspective of time had been so distorted that the days they had been together could have been a lifetime and still he wanted much more. Whilst lying there he wished he could tell her his every thought and that he knew her thoughts too. How often did she think about him? He asked himself knowing that his every waking moment was filled with thoughts of her. Then his mind turned to the day ahead and he imagined what might happen during the day and the night. His mind focussed more and more on the night imagining and fantasising a hundred different scenarios that might lead him to being in her bed once more, and perhaps things might even go a step further. Daniel had to force himself to stop thinking such things, not only in case she did know his thoughts but because the more he contemplated it the more difficult it became not to kiss her and create quite a scene on the beach. At that moment he was very glad they weren't at a nudist beach. Seeing her in her bathing costume drove him crazy enough but any more and he felt that he would lose all of his faculties.

Daniel was not the only one getting restless. Sarah and Jenny had both sat up and been talking.

"I think I'll take a swim," said Sarah.

"I'll join you," said Jenny.

"Me too," said Lisa.

"Don't go out too far there might be some strong currents," warned Daniel.

"Okay," said Sarah.

The three of them ran down to the water and began to play in the clear sea, standing against the waves and splashing each other.

"I think I'll join them," said Phillip.

Daniel and Matthew both watched Phillip follow the same path as the girls towards the sea and wade over to Lisa where he proceeded to pick her up and drop her back down into the water. Lisa was clearly not happy with him and she tried to knock him down but he was prepared and she could not manage it which led to all three of the girls ganging up on him. Together they overpowered him and knocked him into the water. Lisa kept him pinned down until he relented and seemingly surrendered to her.

With that Jenny and Sarah swam away together and left them in peace. Matthew turned to look at Daniel and said,

"It looks like she's got your brother under control."

"That's no mean feat," said Daniel.

"How about you?"

"I'll never have him under control."

"That's not what I meant. You didn't come back last night."

Daniel looked over towards where Jenny was swimming.

"Or the night before, in fact come to think about it..." said Matthew.

"No. Well the thing is-"

"It's okay I think I've a pretty good idea where you've been."

"It's not like that."

"I never said it was."

"I know but I didn't want you thinking I was like Phillip."

"That's why it surprised me. I would have expected something like this from him but not from you."

"We're not... I'm not... It isn't a fling. It's more than that."

"Are you sure?"

"Yes. We've not even, you know?"

"I really don't need to know. I thought your brother's snoring was bad but frankly the other noises are simply disturbing."

"There's an image I never wanted."

"Neither did I."

"It sounds crazy and maybe it is but I've never felt this way before about anyone."

"I can tell."

"You can?"

"It's obvious. Your whole family could see it."

"They could?"

"Of course. Why do you think they were all making such a fuss?"

"I don't know. I mean they are friendly."

"They are but they also know she's special."

"She's incredible."

"I don't know much but if she means so much to you, makes you feel the way you do, then you've got to tell her and make sure you hold on to her for as long as you can."

"How do I do that? Here and now it seems so simple but when we get back. What do I do then? I don't want to lose her."

"Tell her how you feel and if she feels the same you'll make it work."

"I know she feels the same."

"Then the rest is only logistics."

Daniel thought about what he was saying for a moment but there was a trace of doubt in his mind. Something that he thought Jenny had tried to tell him but hadn't.

"Has Sarah or Lisa said anything about us?" asked Daniel.

"No. I don't think Lisa even knows. She's too much like your brother. As for Sarah, well, I think all she wants to do is protect her friend."

"It's just I think there's something..."

At that moment Jenny came back with Sarah. Daniel and Matthew both felt slightly awkward.

"Oh looks like we interrupted something," said Sarah.

"We were just talking," said Matthew.

"Gossiping more like," said Sarah.

"Men do love to gossip," added Jenny.

"Very funny," said Daniel.

He looked at Jenny and wondered if there really was a secret she was keeping and what it could possibly be.

"Aren't they getting a little far out?" said Sarah looking back at Lisa and Phillip.

They all looked and saw that Phillip was twenty metres away from Lisa and moving further out. Daniel got to his feet and ran into the water. He saw Lisa was trying to swim back to the shallower water but struggling. Phillip started to try and swim back too but his efforts weren't getting him anywhere. Looking back Daniel saw that Jenny, Sarah and Matthew were coming towards him. As they watched it became clear that Phillip was caught in a powerful current.

"He's not that strong a swimmer," said Daniel.

Jenny came to his side.

"Go," she said.

"If I get into trouble get help," said Daniel

"I'll help Lisa," said Sarah.

They both ran out as far as they could before they dived into the waves and started swimming and they soon found themselves out of their depth. Sarah swam away from the current towards Lisa but Daniel swam straight into it. It caught him and began to pull him along, at a metre a second, then faster still. He used the current to get him to his brother as fast as he could. As he swam he turned his head and saw that Sarah had already reached Lisa and was helping her back to the safer shallower water. When he looked ahead he saw that Phillip was still quite a distance from him and panicking splashing frantically against the current. Daniel put his face down into the water and pushed himself as hard as he could to reach his brother. The more he swam the more he could feel his muscles working, he tried to breathe in and out as deeply as he could to stave off the lactic acid build up but he had to keep pushing. All he could feel was the sea all around him, the taste of salt in his mouth, the alternating silence and splash of water in his ears, and an awful sense of dread. He knew he should be getting closer to Phillip but every time a wave blocked his vision he feared he would not be able to reach him, and every time he saw him again he was afraid it might be the last time for Phillip was slipping beneath the surface, only to fight all the harder to get back up again. Exhaustion was setting in.

The current continued to propel Daniel and Phillip further out to sea but all that mattered was that he reached his brother and kept him afloat. As he got closer he could hear Phillip's gurgled shouts and soon he was right by his side. Phillip stretched out to grab Daniel and took hold of his arm. Daniel swam behind him and kicked with his legs to keep his exhausted brother above the surface and told him to stop fighting or he would drown them both. It took a minute for Phillip to calm down enough and by that point he was too fatigued to fight either the current or Daniel. Daniel looked back towards the shore and could see the whole horseshoe bay. He did not want to get pulled any further out and so he began to swim perpendicular to the current until he could feel that they were free of it but the safety of the beach was a long way off. He had to try and get back without being pushed too close to the rocky edges and so he told his brother to gently kick his legs and together they made a slow but steady pace back to the shallows where all their friends and several concerned beach goers were waiting for them. Matthew helped get Phillip back onto the beach whilst Jenny could not wait for Daniel to stand up before checking on him.

"Are you all right?" she asked.

"I am now."

He looked over towards his brother who was receiving a lot of attention from Lisa. Daniel got back onto his feet and Jenny offered him her support which he took. They went over to Phillip.

"We're both very lucky. I hope you realise that?" said Daniel.

"Yeah I know," said Phillip.

"I told you not to go so far out."

"I never heard you say that."

"You're quite unbelievable, you know that?"

"Yes I am."

They remained at Għajn Tuffieħa until the swimmers had all recovered and then they headed back towards Golden Bay where they found somewhere to eat and replenish their energy. After lunch Phillip was back to his old self and it seemed as if nothing had happened.

"Should we head back to the hotel?" asked Lisa.

"Why?" said Phillip.

"Because you nearly drowned."

"No I'm fine. We've got places to go and see, right little brother?"

"Sure."

"You know if I have my geography correct then it isn't too far to Anchor Bay," said Phillip.

"It isn't a bay full of anchors is it?" asked Lisa.

"Now how did you know that?"

"Just a lucky guess I suppose."

"It's not a bay full of anchors," said Daniel.

"Oh," said Lisa.

"It's about an hour north of here on foot," said Daniel.

"Well if you two are okay then I don't mind going," said Matthew.

"I don't mind the walk," said Jenny.

"That's fine with me," said Sarah.

With them all in agreement they walked north-west following the tracks and trails through an area of the island that was almost untouched with a mixture of habitats from the cliff top garigue with its mixture of evergreen shrubs, aromatic herbs and bunch grasses to boulder screes with the only signs of man's influence some small fields and the occasional farm building. As they walked they separated out with Phillip and Lisa at the back, Sarah and Jenny in the middle and Matthew and Daniel in the lead.

"We never finished our conversation earlier," said Matthew.

"No. I guess we didn't," said Daniel.

Daniel looked behind and saw that Jenny and Sarah were talking. He listened but could not make out what they were saying.

"It has all happened so quickly," said Daniel.

"Is that a bad thing?"

"No. I didn't expect it. I thought the three of us would have some fun on holiday together. I never thought I'd…"

"Why do we have such a problem saying how we feel?"

"Because we're men and Englishmen at that."

"That we are but sometimes even men have to articulate their feelings, even get a little mushy."

"I'm not very good at it."

"None of us are. It is hard to say and hard to hear. We

can't understand why anyone would love us when we find it hard to love ourselves."

Daniel recognised too much of what Matthew was saying. He thought back to when Jenny had said she loved him. How vulnerable she had been and how much of a jerk he felt for not telling her properly then and there that he felt the same way.

"How do you think Phillip does it?" asked Daniel.

"I don't know."

"I couldn't hook up with someone and then never see them again afterwards."

"I couldn't do it either."

"Do you think they have feelings for each other?"

"I don't have a clue. They seem to live in the moment without a thought of the consequences that tomorrow might bring."

"At times I wish I could be more like that."

"I think you and Jenny are doing a pretty good job of being spontaneous so far."

"I wish I had your confidence. Most of the time I'm terrified I'm going to screw things up."

"Most of us are. Well I am at least."

"Not Phillip though."

"No I guess not and he's lucky he had you to deal with his consequences. This morning proved that."

"We were both lucky. You can't fight nature."

"Yet you did."

"Not really."

"All I can say is that standing on shore, watching you out there, well I didn't know what to do."

"Yeah but you can't swim."

"That's not the point. The point is you knew what you had to do and you did it and I'm sure if you follow those same instincts with Jenny then everything will work out for you both."

"You really think so?"

"I saw her reaction when you were in the water, she could not have been more concerned for you. I had to hold her back from going in after you."

"She tried to follow us in?"

"Without a moment's hesitation."

"I didn't know."

"You were preoccupied. All I'm telling you is to let things happen between the two of you. Don't look for things to sabotage yourselves. There are too many problems in the world without searching them out."

Daniel knew he was right, he was searching for problems where none existed beyond those of his own making. All he had to do was be honest and allow himself to enjoy the time they had left together. Beyond that he did not want or have to think about it.

"I feel bad for having bailed on you yesterday," said Daniel.

"You did leave us a note. That's more than your brother would have done."

"We all came together though and we don't get to see each other that often."

"That's the way of things. As I said before don't go looking for a problem where there isn't one."

"So we're good?"

"Of course, although your brother is kind of exhausting."

"Are we talking a couple of drinks in reparations or more?"

"Maybe just the one."

"What did he do?"

"He took us on the scenic version of a walk again."

"He was lost again?"

"Yes, not that he ever admits it, or stops for directions, or to actually look at a map. You do know where you're going right?"

"Yes."

"That's more than he did, he dragged us all over the place and I swear he was making all kinds of things up to impress Lisa and Sarah."

"He kind of does that. It's more a re-imagined retelling of some half fact."

"Well we still managed to have a good day but I kind of think Sarah might want to spend a little more time with her friends."

They both looked back and saw how close Jenny and Sarah looked.

"Maybe we should give them some space," said Daniel, though he really did not want to be apart from Jenny.

"It might be an idea, though I'm not sure how well your brother will take it."

"We should catch up with our family a bit more."

"That sounds like a plan."

"What about you? I don't want you to feel like we're bailing on you again."

"To tell you the truth I'd kind of like a break from Phillip."

Daniel laughed and understood only too well. They both waited for Jenny and Sarah to catch up.

"We were talking about what we might like to do for with the rest of the week," said Matthew.

"We've been talking about it too," said Jenny. "Sarah would like to take one of those harbour cruises but I know you're not so good with boats," she said to Daniel.

Daniel looked at her and could see that she wanted to stay with him and he was glad.

"We have a family thing tomorrow," said Daniel, "and we can always meet in the evening at the hotel?"

"Of course we can. Can't we Sarah?" asked Jenny.

"Yes you can," said Sarah giving them both her blessing.

The four of them carried on walking together, with Phillip and Lisa trailing further behind, until the track they were following took them past an observation tower and then joined with a narrow road. They followed the road until they reached the bay across from which they saw a small village.

"Welcome to Sweethaven," said Daniel.

"It looks like a ghost town," said Jenny.

The small village was made up of a group of rustic and ramshackle buildings that were in disrepair. The signs on the buildings were faded and there didn't appear to be anyone else around.

"Let's go and walk around, and all will be revealed," said Daniel.

They followed him around the bay overlooking Sweethaven and then they turned and went down from the cliffs and into the village itself. The closer they got the more the details began to appear, the wooden buildings were all different colours, the pitched roofs were shingled, and each building had peculiar quirks including balconies on the roofs which could only be accessed by climbing up the roof on a steep ladder. As they entered the village Jenny was the first to realise that none of it was real.

"It's not a real village," said Jenny.

"No, it was a film set," said Daniel.

"They built this whole village for a film?" asked Sarah.

"Yes for a movie version of Popeye."

"There was a film of Popeye?"

"Yes back at the beginning of the eighties and they left all this behind. One day it'll probably be a theme park but for now we can go wherever we like."

Even though the place was in disrepair they began to see past it and they became immersed in the fictional village of Sweethaven, exploring the buildings and the docks, taking silly photos of themselves at the carnival cut outs of Popeye, Olive Oyl, Swee'Pea, Bluto and Wimpy until they were all played out. It took them half an hour to walk from Anchor Bay to the bus stop. They were glad of the public transportation but the roads were bumpy and the bus rickety which made them feel the toll of the day. After an hour and half they were happy to be off the bus and back at the hotel, more so to find that the lift was working again. They all dined together and the girls finalised their plans for the next day whilst the boys pretended that they knew what they were doing. Phillip wanted to go to the bar but Lisa, Sarah and Matthew all said they were done for the night. Daniel could tell Jenny was finished as well but Phillip continued trying to press Daniel to go with him and so Jenny wished them both goodnight and went up to her room. The two brothers went into the bar and whilst Phillip got a couple of drinks for them both he did not seem interested in drinking it. He wanted to talk to Daniel but it took him a while before he felt comfortable enough to move beyond a little small talk.

"I'm glad we could get away from everyone for a little while," said Phillip.

"I thought you thrived on social activity?"

"Yeah, that's kind of the problem. Did you know that

Lisa and I hooked up?"

"I had noticed."

"I don't think we should have."

"Oh?"

"Yeah I know. I wasn't thinking. At least not with what matters."

"I don't know what to say."

"That's the problem. Neither do we and today kind of put things in perspective. Sometimes I don't listen and it gets me in trouble and at some point well..."

"You'll always be fine."

"Probably but the thing is everything between Lisa and me was fake, nothing but the machinations of alcohol and we both thought we were okay with that."

"But you're not?"

"She isn't and I don't want to be."

"So you can go your separate ways."

"We already have."

"When did that happen?"

"Today after the beach. We said we'd exchange numbers, remain friends and you know be amicable."

"That's good isn't it?"

"It isn't what I want. I want something more."

"From her?"

"In general."

"You'll find it. I know you will."

"I hope so. I wanted you to know though in case things got awkward between us."

Phillip pushed his drink away.

"I'm kind of tired I guess, nearly drowning kind of exhausted me," said Phillip.

"Yeah, it exhausted me too."

Daniel took a few sips from his drink and then they

left the bar and headed back to their room. Phillip went straight to bed and was soon asleep. Matthew and Daniel could both hear him snoring but Daniel wanted to go and see Jenny. He wondered if she was still awake. The only way he would find out was to go and see. Daniel left his room and went down a few floors and to Jenny's door. He softly knocked on the door, wanting it to be loud enough for her to hear but not so loud that he would wake her if she was already sleeping. The door opened swiftly and Jenny pulled him inside.

## CHAPTER EIGHT

Jenny lay on top of Daniel and he slowly woke up.

"Breakfast," she said.

He looked around and saw that Jenny had brought up a tray for him. She rolled off him and brought the tray over. Daniel sat up and rubbed the sleep from his eyes.

"I have to go now. We're catching the boat in a few minutes," said Jenny.

"Okay. Thank you for breakfast," said Daniel taking a bite of toast.

Jenny stood and watched.

"What? A crumb?" said Daniel wiping his mouth with the napkin.

"No. I'm just looking."

"Is something wrong?"

"Absolutely nothing. You're cute in the morning."

"Only in the morning?"

"Maybe. I'll have to see you tonight to know for sure,"

said Jenny as she checked her watch and knew she had to run. "Have a good day, I'll see you later," she said making her way to the door.

"Jenny."

She paused.

"I love you," said Daniel.

"I know," she said smiling broadly and leaving.

The thought of Daniel lying in her bed kept her in good spirits as she, Sarah and Lisa caught the boat tour from Sliema. The boat took them out of Sliema and past the entrance to the Grand Harbour and then onwards towards Marsakala Bay and around the coast of the island. The three of them stood looking over the side as the boat took them in and around the bays at a leisurely pace. When they came to the south of the island the tour guide said they were coming to Pretty Bay and Jenny saw the reason why Daniel's aunt had said it was not so pretty any more. There was an enormous port. She found it fascinating, to see the giant cranes loading and unloading mountains of cargo containers to ships that appeared too large to believe they could float. On the opposite side from the port was a power station which made the whole area seem very industrial. The guide's description of approaching the largest fishing village made all three of them think they were touring an industrial estate, which was not quite the tour they had in mind. Once they were past the power station they began to see the fishing village of Marsaxlokk which stood in stark contrast to its neighbours. The village was quite picturesque as was St. George's Bay and Pretty Bay as long as they blocked the port and other industrial works from their minds and view.

Jenny and Sarah were happy when they heard that the

next stop would be the Blue Grotto. The name instantly brought back the memory of the earlier part of their holiday. They looked at each other and then at Lisa and hoped that she would enjoy the experience as much as they had.

"Hard to believe that was only last week isn't it?" said Sarah.

"It feels like it was months ago. How strange is that?" said Jenny.

"I wonder if we'll see Rocco again. He was a lot of fun."

"Who's Rocco?" asked Lisa.

"Daniel's uncle," said Jenny.

"Oh."

"He took us on a tour whilst you were recovering one day," said Sarah.

Lisa shuddered with the thought of her hangover from that day.

"Now we all get to see it together," said Jenny hugging both her friends.

As they passed the caves Jenny and Sarah told Lisa what it was like inside them, how clear the water was in one and how colourful it was in another. Lisa peered at the caves but she could only catch a glimpse of what her friends were trying to describe.

"I suppose you had to be there," said Lisa.

"This isn't the upbeat Lisa we know and love," said Sarah.

They stood back from the sides and sat on the nearby seats still watching the coast go by. Jenny took Lisa's hand and asked,

"What's the matter?"

"I make bad choices when I'm drunk… and when I'm

sober."

For a moment Jenny wondered if Daniel's brother could be that bad. She asked herself how different from Daniel could he be?

"It's not Phillip," said Lisa, "he was fine but we're not a good match."

"So you part ways and don't look back," said Sarah.

"We decided we'd stay friends," said Lisa.

"That's good isn't it?" asked Jenny.

"It is but I wish I didn't keep repeating the same mistakes. A man shows an interest and I jump into bed with him and my head fills with ideas that he's the one; that we'll get married and live happily ever after."

Jenny drifted in her own thoughts, thinking about Daniel. She could imagine marrying him and she knew they would be happy. Lisa looked at her.

"I'm sorry," said Lisa. "I'm being selfish."

"No you're not," said Jenny.

"We came away to forget about men and everything else."

"What else should we talk about then?" Jenny asked kindly.

"I don't know," said Lisa. "Maybe we should just enjoy the tour and a little wine."

Lisa got up and went to fetch them all a glass.

"A few glasses of wine and she'll bounce right back," said Sarah.

"Isn't that repeating the same pattern though?" asked Jenny

"It is and she'll probably keep making the same mistakes again."

"Don't we all?"

"I hope that we learn something."

"Maybe, if you're lucky."

"And if not?"

"Then you remain stuck in a vicious circle."

"And what happens if you break the cycle?" asked Sarah.

"I'm not sure we ever truly do," said Jenny.

"Why not?"

"I think it's our nature."

"To continually screw up?"

"To be lazy and let ourselves remain trapped."

"Is that how you feel, trapped?"

"I did. Until…"

"Until Daniel."

"Yes."

"Even though?"

"Even though it can't last?"

"Well, yes."

"I don't know if it matters, at least not at the moment."

"But what about when we have to go back?"

"I don't know. I haven't found a way to tell him and I guess the truth is all I want to do is enjoy our time together. For all of us to enjoy our time together. Okay?"

"Yes, of course. That's why we're here isn't it? To have fun and enjoy ourselves."

"It is."

A part of her could not help but think what would happen once the holiday was over but she constantly tried to push that to the back of her mind. Jenny was enjoying living in the moment with her friends and with Daniel. If she could then she would make it last forever but reality never seemed to allow for such things. Her mind filled with thoughts of Daniel and she could not wait to get back and see him again. Her train of thought was only broken when Lisa returned with wine.

"Well here's to us," said Lisa.

They clinked their glasses together and sampled the local wine.

"To learning from mistakes," said Sarah looking at Lisa.

Lisa sipped her wine, attempting moderation, whilst the tour guide announced,

"We're now travelling along Dingli Cliffs, a particularly romantic location for all you couples especially at sunset, when you could walk hand in hand or simply stop and look out over the sea."

On hearing the guide Lisa took a bigger drink of her wine and they all looked up at the cliffs which appeared impassable from the boat. The sheer rock was a stark contrast to the warmth and joy of the people they had met. Jenny looked away from the cliffs and out to the open sea.

"It's hard to imagine going back," she said.

"Yes it is," said Sarah.

"You don't have to think about it yet," said Lisa. "Now drink up."

Lisa waited, a little impatiently, for them both to finish and then went to fetch another round.

"We'll be drunk before lunch," said Sarah.

"I think that's her plan," said Jenny.

"Well let's try and slow her down, okay?"

"I don't like our chances. She's a force of nature."

"I know but I'd like be able to walk back to the hotel."

Lisa came back with more wine, her own glass already half drunk.

The tour guide announced the next points of interest which included the beach they were at yesterday and not long after that Popeye's Village. By the time they stopped at the island of Comino Lisa had discovered alcohol made the movement and motion of the boat far more pronounced and was clinging to the railing, as if they had been in a turbulent storm. Despite Lisa's imbalance the water in Comino's Blue Lagoon was placid and a rich azure colour that contrasted with the surrounding deeper blue sea. Jenny and Sarah pried Lisa away from the railings and tried to convince her to have lunch but failed. They set her ashore to find her feet whilst they ate and then they joined her to sunbathe and paddle in the water, before it was time to make the return leg of the tour. The boat headed back past Mellieha Bay, St. Paul's Island, the casino, St. Julian's Bay and as they passed each place Jenny remembered the time they had spent there, the things Daniel had told her and all that they had seen together. When they drifted back into Sliema in the early evening she had begun to daydream. She thought of Daniel continuously, he had invaded every part of her thoughts, dreams and even her nightmares. Jenny looked towards Valletta and wondered if Daniel was there at that moment, she felt certain that he was. She closed her eyes and breathed in the clean sea air until it filled her lungs and as she slowly exhaled it felt as if she was breathing out life. When she breathed in again she felt that same life energy return and she realised how enchanted she was with the island and Daniel. She felt as if there was a strange magic to the place and to him and it had her completely under their spell. When Jenny opened her eyes she saw the now familiar sights of the high street of Sliema.

As they left the boat behind and walked back towards the hotel Jenny was still thinking about their time on the island so far. The trip around the coast had been like a recap of her time there. So many beautiful places and moments that Jenny could not forget but like any recap the day's outing had been devoid of something. It hadn't been new. It was a retelling of the story so far. A story that had become very much about the two of them and without Daniel the day had felt incomplete. She missed his presence; being able to be close to him, to touch him and sense him. Jenny turned to look out across the bay at Valletta and imagined him there with his family. Her gaze returned to the path back to the hotel but her mind was thinking of her own family back in England. She wondered what they would think of him and she wished that they could meet. Maybe if they had met a year ago then things could have been different. But then she wondered if they had met under different circumstances would they have fallen for each other? Jenny hoped that they would have. She knew it was nothing but a what if and all what ifs are dangerous. They are idle speculation about events that have passed and can never be changed. Only right there at that moment was she free. More free than she had ever been. Away from everything and everyone but her closest friends. She had cut loose the bonds that tied her and soared up into the heavens.

They stopped near the hotel and bought a few soft drinks from a small kiosk. The sun appeared to be in decline, slowly bringing the end of the day. Jenny was still half lost in her own thoughts but Lisa brought her back to earth.

"Here you go," said Lisa handing her a glass bottle.

"Thank you," said Jenny.

"You've been miles away all afternoon," said Sarah.

"Sorry. I was daydreaming."

"About what?" asked Lisa.

"About Daniel of course," said Sarah.

Jenny gently bit her bottom lip.

"Why?" asked Lisa.

"Because." said Sarah.

"What? Oh, you and Daniel have been?" said Lisa intimating something unseemly.

"No. It's not like that."

"Well I never expected anything like this from you," said Lisa.

"Don't tease her," said Sarah.

"I think I should."

"No you shouldn't."

"Why not?"

"Because this isn't the same."

"It isn't?" said Lisa looking at Jenny. "Oh no. You love him."

"I've never felt like this before," said Jenny.

"Well your timing is awful."

"Lisa!" said Sarah rebuking her.

"I'm sorry but it's true."

"She's right, my timing is terrible," said Jenny.

"Does he feel the same?" asked Lisa.

"Yes."

"But you haven't told him?"

"No."

"Oh god," said Lisa, hugging Jenny and stepping away.

"She's worried about you. We both are," said Sarah.

"I know," said Jenny, "but can't I enjoy it while it lasts?"

"Of course you can," Sarah hugged her, "but you have to tell him."

"I know," said Jenny, "but isn't any kind of love a

good thing?"

"I hope so."

Lisa came back to them and said,

"Tell me everything."

"I will," said Jenny.

"I can't believe I didn't see this," said Lisa.

"You were preoccupied," said Sarah teasing her.

The three of them continued walking back to the hotel where they were greeted by the receptionist.

"Good evening, we have a message for you," the receptionist said passing a note to Jenny.

"What is it?" asked Lisa.

"Daniel's uncle called. It says the boys are in trouble and he needs our help."

"What kind of trouble?" said Sarah.

"It doesn't say. Only to come to his home."

"What should we do?" asked Lisa.

"I don't know but if Daniel is in trouble..."

"I'm sure he's okay," said Sarah.

"I have to go to him," said Jenny.

"We'll all go," said Sarah.

They left the hotel and walked along the promenade and found a taxi. They gave the taxi driver the address and both Jenny and Sarah soon recognised the streets leading to Rocco's house. The cab pulled up and they saw Rocco outside, puffing away on a cigarette. His face lit up as soon as he saw them and he came over and paid the taxi driver.

"I'm so glad you came," said Rocco.

"What's the matter?" asked Jenny. "Is Daniel all right?"

"Come, I take you to them."

They followed Rocco inside and could hear a lot of people talking, chatting and laughing as they went upstairs to the main living area. Jenny recognised several of Daniel's family members and then she saw Daniel, Phillip and Matthew all sat together in a line on the settee.

"See how sad they are?" said Rocco.

Jenny looked at him and then at Daniel who saw her and lit up instantly.

"And now he is better," said Rocco.

Phillip and Matthew also brightened up when they saw Sarah and Lisa. Jenny looked around.

"You're having a party?"

"Yes, yes," said Rocco, "and they were all so sad; I didn't know what to do but then I thought about you and I knew. So now you all eat, drink and be happy, yes?"

Jenny felt her concern disappearing as Daniel came over to her. He was okay. Not really in trouble.

"What are you doing here?" asked Daniel.

"I guess your uncle invited us," said Jenny looking at Rocco.

"It is okay?" said Rocco.

"It is okay," said Jenny checking with Sarah and Lisa who nodded their acceptance.

Charlotte saw her new guests and came over and gave the three of them a warm welcome.

"I'm so glad you came," she said hugging and kissing them all. "Now let me fix you something to eat."

She took Sarah's and Lisa's hands and took them over to a large spread of food and began piling their plates. Jenny watched as Phillip went over to Lisa and eagerly started on his next serving. Rocco disappeared back downstairs, presumably to finish his cigarette. Charlotte was waving at her to come over and get something to eat.

"You'd better get a plate," said Daniel.

"I'm not all that hungry," said Jenny.

"You have to eat I'm afraid. It's compulsory at these things."

"Is it a party?"

"An engagement party for one of my cousins."

"Well now I feel like we're crashing the party."

"On the contrary the more people the better."

Charlotte returned to Jenny.

"You're not eating?" she asked.

"Well I…"

"Oh you're too skinny, Daniel come, both of you eat, eat. It's a party and we must celebrate."

They followed Charlotte over to the buffet where Daniel's aunt proceeded to load both of their plates high.

"That's better," said Charlotte assessing her handy work and then leaving to check on her other guests.

Jenny looked at the large pile of food and felt overwhelmed by the quantity.

"Come on," said Daniel taking her over to a table, where he procured two chairs for them both and they sat down.

"I thought you were in trouble," said Jenny.

Daniel did not understand.

"Your uncle called the hotel and left a message," she explained.

"That's Rocco and I'm glad he did. I missed you today."

"Did you really?"

"I did."

"Because I was thinking about you too…"

"And?"

"Now we're together again."

Daniel raised his glass and extended it towards her and she chinked her glass against his.

"To being together," said Daniel.

Jenny smiled at him and tried to find her appetite. As they ate she looked around the room a little more. Sarah and Lisa were sat with a group including Phillip and Matthew and seemed to be fielding questions on where they were from and what it was like there. In another group she saw another one of Daniel's uncles and some familiar faces from the previous gathering.

"Where are your grandparents?" she asked him.

"They said the party should be for the younger people but in truth I don't think my Grandmother was feeling well today."

"I'm sorry to hear that. I hope she feels better soon."

"She will be but it is getting more difficult for her to get out and about as much as she used to. We'll check in on them tomorrow. Maybe you'd like to come with me?"

"I'd love to. I really liked them both."

"I'm glad."

"You'll have to introduce the three of us to your cousin as well. We should congratulate them."

"I will, but first you have to clear your plate or my aunt will force feed you."

"Very funny."

"No really you have to eat."

Jenny continued grazing through the contents of her plate whilst watching Daniel and everyone around her. Eventually she figured out who the engaged couple were as they were the focal point of everyone's attention. Her mind began to imagine what it might be like to be engaged to someone you loved. She fantasised that she might be engaged to Daniel and wondered how he would have proposed. Jenny imagined him proposing to her there in Malta, perhaps at the Upper Barrakka or better still the more private and intimate secret little garden they had visited. Whilst still in her own little fantasy she looked at her hand and could almost feel the metal pressing against her skin as he slipped the ring over her finger. Her mind brought her back to the present and she saw that her ring finger was bare. It had been a pleasant daydream yet she felt it could almost be real. As Jenny gazed upon the faces of so many people she knew that they were all one large community. A group of friends, relatives and neighbours who had come together to forge a family all celebrating happy news. It seemed almost beyond Jenny's comprehension that anyone or any two people could set all their doubts aside and make a commitment to each other that they would spend the rest of their lives together. Until Jenny had met Daniel she would never have thought it truly possible. She feared that people only ever settled. Accepting there was no true love. You convinced yourself how little you could live with, that love could grow or be transferred. In Daniel she had found something quite different. Someone that filled her with desire but more than lust he was the person she wanted to spend her life with, to share her life with. Jenny could feel her love for him as a tangible and real thing living within her. At that moment she wished they were the happy couple looking forward to their lives together. That they could continue being swept up in the whirlwind and elope together and leave everything behind them except their own happiness.

Charlotte returned to check on Jenny and Daniel and was pleased to see both their plates were nearly empty. She sat down next to Daniel.

"I'll put some meat on your bones yet," said Charlotte to Daniel squeezing his arm.

"I'd keep eating if I wasn't so full," said Daniel.

"Are you full too?" she asked Jenny.

"Completely, thank you so much for having us."

"We're glad you came. These boys were moping without you."

"Were they now?" asked Jenny.

"He likes you a lot, you know?" said Charlotte.

"I know."

"You make a nice couple," said Charlotte, "maybe soon we have another party?"

Jenny felt herself blush and saw Daniel's face redden.

"Ah, you see. You both know it is good," said Charlotte reverberating with delight at the idea of another engagement and wedding.

Jenny bit down on her bottom lip and looked up at Daniel who was clearly uncertain what to say or to do. Charlotte saw the effect she was having on them both.

"You're embarrassed? No, no you're too young to be embarrassed and I'm too old to care. If you love each other then you show it. Too many ugly things in the world, so we all need to see the good things. To share the happiness."

"It's just new," said Daniel.

Charlotte reached over Daniel and took Jenny's hand and put it into his whilst keeping her own hand on top.

"Every day is new, and so you show her how you feel every day and you tell her. Yes?"

"Yes," said Jenny and Daniel.

"Oh this is a very good day. Now I go and see if I can make your brother and friend smile too," said Charlotte leaving them still holding hands.

Jenny looked at Daniel and saw he was sniggering like a child who knew he shouldn't find something funny but couldn't help it. It was infectious.

The engagement party went on long into the night. Jenny could not help but be taken in by the atmosphere and with it she began to recall all the events that had brought them to that point. She thought about how they had explored the islands and their feelings for each other. By the time they had returned to their hotel she knew that she had found her soul mate. The thought of returning to London without him felt like it would completely shatter her. In a haze everyone else was gone and Daniel was standing at the entrance to her hotel room door. She leaned into him pressing her hands against his chest.

"What would you like to do?" asked Jenny.

"Now?" asked Daniel his voice trembled.

"Or a little later."

"I don't know. What do you want to do?"

"I'm willing to follow your lead. For a little while longer at least."

Jenny looked at him and could tell he was uncomfortable as if struggling with his first crush. She slid her hands down his chest and took Daniel's hands and put them around her and slowly stepped backwards, pulling him inside her room and then pushing him back into the door closing it. Her body pressed against his and she kissed him, tenderly and softly. Letting him know it was okay, that she trusted him and wanted him to take control. Still he hesitated.

"Show me how you feel," whispered Jenny.

"I… I can't."

"Why not?"

"I don't want anything to change between us."

"Some changes are better."

"I don't want to lose you."

"You won't."

She looked at him and could see his struggle was paralysing him. His hand was on the door handle as if he wanted to bolt.

"Don't you want me?" she asked.

"I do. I really do."

"Then come away from the door."

He stepped towards her, his hand letting the door handle slip out of reach.

"Why don't you sit down," said Jenny.

Daniel obeyed her and sat on the settee.

"I'll be right back," she said.

Jenny went into the bedroom and closed the doors before going into the bathroom. She could feel her heart pounding in her chest as she pulled off her clothes and changed into a black nightgown and robe. Her mind was filled with the possibilities of what might happen and she was almost overwhelmed with an anxious excitement. It felt like a tremendous risk. Daniel had been so nervous, he hadn't even touched her and now she was about to make herself completely vulnerable to him. She was terrified that he wouldn't want her. That he would think there was something wrong with her and reject her. It took every bit of her bravery to leave the bathroom and open the bedroom doors. Her first fear was alleviated. Daniel was still there and she most definitely had his attention. Slowly Jenny loosened the bow on her robe, until it opened revealing the nightgown. He was watching her intently but what she really wanted was for him to come to her, to kiss her, to love her. She waited. He remained static, his hands tightly gripping the seat cushion as if to let go would cause him to lose control but that was what Jenny wanted. To entice him further she slipped out of the robe. The cooler air touched her skin where the robe had been but still she felt her skin burning. Daniel remained seated but she could see that he was struggling.

"What's the matter?" she asked him.

"You're so beautiful."

"Come to me."

He bridged the distance between them swiftly, his eyes locked on hers. Gently he put his arms around her and pulled her to him. She draped her arms around his neck. She could not tell if it was his heart pounding or her own, his breath or hers. He kissed her. His hands moved over her back and pressed her body tighter against his as their passions increased.

"Are you sure?" he asked her his breathing already heavy.

"Yes."

Daniel pulled off his own shirt and Jenny traced her hand over the contours of his stomach and the small scar on his abdomen. He twitched nervously when she touched the wound, backing away a little. Jenny stopped him.

"It's okay."

"I know."

"I love you."

"I love you too."

They kissed again and moved over to the bed where Jenny lay down and watched as Daniel began to remove the rest of his clothes.

CHAPTER NINE

Daniel was fixed to the settee, anchoring himself by gripping the seat cushion as hard as he could but his gaze was fixed on Jenny. She looked beautiful and he wanted to go over to her but he was afraid of the carnal thoughts stirring within him. He didn't want to lose control but when she said,

"Come to me."

He could not help himself and he went to her to hold her and kiss her. The feel of her body pressed against his made him lose all sense of everything else but her. All he could think of was her, how good she looked and felt, the scent of her hair, the taste of her lips. The last bastion of his self-restraint was crumbling but he had to know this was what she wanted, as silly as it seemed in that moment, he had to ask.

"Are you sure?"

"Yes," said Jenny.

Feeling a surge of adrenaline he pulled off his shirt. He felt her hands running over his stomach but he flinched when she touched his scar. In his mind he cursed himself for his reaction. Backing away was the last thing he wanted to do.

"It's okay," she said.

"I know," he said feeling a tremendous relief that she hadn't been offended somehow.

"I love you," said Jenny.

"I love you too."

It had never been so true, he felt, for she seemed to overlook all of his faults and flaws, even his insecurities, and that made him love her all the more. He kissed Jenny again and they moved over to the bed. She lay down. Her nightgown hardly covered the top of her thighs, and the lace like pattern on her chest intimated and teased the shape of her breasts. It was a truly exciting and terrifying moment as he removed his own clothes. He was not used to being naked in front of anyone and he was afraid that somehow seeing him like that would push her away but she hardly stopped looking into his eyes. Jenny sat up a little to kiss him. He supported her as they lay down together their lips still touching, their breathing merged. She pressed her lips up against his kissing him more passionately and inflaming him further. Her hands ran down his back and then around his hips. Daniel had to draw back for air. His head was spinning, his skin tingled and he wanted to feel her flesh against his. He ran his hands up over her thighs and began to push the nightgown away. Jenny arched her back so it slipped up over her stomach and then she sat up a little so he could remove it completely. Daniel felt his nerves fade away and held her as he was consumed by their passion. He never wanted to let her go and he didn't until late the next morning.

Daniel watched Jenny. She was lying half on her side with her hands beneath her head acting as a pillow. He traced the line of her spine with his fingers up to her neck and then brushed her hair from her face. As he looked at her the sheets draped over her like a flowing white gown. Her skin was soft and smooth to his touch. He wanted to protect her, to ensure she could always sleep so peacefully. The sun's rays pushed through the curtains and made her skin glow. Daniel held her again and she began to wake. Turning from her side to her back, in his arms, she opened her eyes to look at him.

"I missed you yesterday," said Jenny.

"I missed you too," said Daniel. "But we're together now."

"Yes we are," said Jenny absorbing their situation.

"Is this kind of crazy?"

"It is but it is a good kind of crazy I think."

"I've never felt this way before."

"Neither have I."

"Is it okay that I'm utterly in love with you?"

"I don't mind," said Jenny kissing him and then moving to sit up on the edge of the bed.

Daniel watched her, he couldn't help but glimpse the side of her breasts and he was filled with desire for her once more. He moved over to her and held her.

"Do you think you will ever feel like this again?" asked Jenny.

"What do you mean?"

"Do you think you would ever love someone else?"

Daniel felt her slump slightly in his arms and he did not really know what to say.

"I don't know. I never expected to fall in love but I have. With you."

Jenny held his hands.

"What's the matter? Did you have another bad dream?" asked Daniel

"No. I slept better than I have in a long time."

Daniel moved so he could see her face. Jenny looked at him with such love and happiness that it almost hid the speck of sadness in her eyes.

"You know I'd do anything for you?"

"That's sweet," said Jenny.

"I mean it. I'll do anything you ask if it makes you happy. You only have to tell me."

"I will," she said and kissed him.

They both got dressed and as they were about to leave the room Jenny saw a note pushed under the door.

"It appears we have the day to ourselves," said Jenny showing Daniel the note which he saw was from Lisa and signed with hugs and kisses. "What would you like to do?" she asked.

Daniel kissed Jenny's neck and wrapped his hands around her waist.

"Besides that," she said turning and kissing him back.

"Well…"

"You did say you were going to check on your grandmother."

"Yes. We should do that."

"Yes we should."

"We could just make it before the siesta starts if we go now."

"Then let's go," said Jenny taking his hand and leading him from the room, the hotel and to the bus stop and on to Valletta.

The sun was shining, the temperature perfect and everything about Jenny was incredible and it made Daniel feel on top of the world. They moved through the city with ease and soon they were outside his grandparent's building, distinguished by the columns straddling the entrance. They climbed the first steps into the building and inside the familiar smell instantly greeted him along with the sight of all the stairs to the top.

"They live on the top floor," Daniel told Jenny.

"There's no lift?"

"No."

"I'll race you to the top then."

Before Daniel could say anything Jenny ran up the first flight of steps. Daniel chased after her but she had a good lead on him. Even when she slowed to pull off her shoes she managed to stay in the lead and he chased her to the top floor. Their footsteps echoed all over the building. When Daniel reached the flat he saw that Jenny had continued to go up one more floor to the roof. Taking the opportunity to catch his breath, Daniel walked around and saw her looking out of breath at the top of the stairs, still with her shoes in her hand. He beckoned her to come back down, which she did and then leaned on him whilst she put her shoes back on. They walked to the door together and Daniel rang the doorbell. Inside they heard someone approaching. The bolt clunked as it was pulled back and the door creaked on its hinges as it was opened. William looked out and upon seeing who it was his face lit up with a big rosy smile.

"Vi, Vi, we have company," he called opening the door for them to step inside.

"Hi grandad, we thought we'd check in on you. How are you?"

"We're well."

"And gran?"

"She's better today."

"That's good."

"You've swapped your brother?"

"Yes I traded Phillip for Jenny."

"I think you got a good deal."

Daniel saw his grandmother coming out from the bedroom. They went along the hallway to meet her. She greeted them both with a hug and a kiss on both cheeks.

"I was getting ready for a siesta," she said.

"We're sorry," said Jenny.

"No, no," said Violet, "it isn't time yet. Come in, come in. William fix them some tea."

Daniel looked at his grandfather and saw that he wasn't going to argue. He went with him and helped him make a large pot of tea and then carried it back to the living room. Jenny and Violet were looking over a few family albums that had been pulled from a large stack under a side table. Daniel handed out the tea cups and poured before sitting down in one of the large armchairs. He watched and listened as his grandmother showed Jenny his ancestors, his great grandparents, his grandparents, his father's generation and then his own through a series of christenings, confirmations, weddings and family portraits.

"There's a strong resemblance between you and your grandfather," said Jenny.

"Do you think so?" said William.

"I can see it."

"Ah, I always thought Daniel was a good looking boy," said William.

"He's cute," said Jenny embarrassing him further.

"You know you can see the hotel from the window," said Daniel changing the subject.

"Really?" asked Jenny.

"Oh you haven't seen?" said William. "Vi let her look."

Violet took the album from Jenny's lap and she went to the far window. The view allowed her to see all the way over to Sliema. William and Daniel came over to her and William pointed out where their hotel was. Both Daniel and Jenny stood and looked out for a few minutes. William returned to his seat and began pouring everyone more tea.

"Now a little more tea," he said.

Daniel's grandmother had changed seats leaving Daniel and Jenny to sit on the settee together.

"How was the party?" asked Violet.

"Very good, a lot of food and it went on quite late," said Daniel.

"Ah your aunt always puts out a good spread," said William.

"She does," agreed Daniel.

"Now, Jenny," said William, "if I remember you were from London?"

"Yes that's right."

"Ah a big city. We got lost there once didn't we Vi?"

Violet nodded.

"Which part are you from?"

"South of the river, not too far from Battersea," said Jenny.

"Yes? I remember the big power station and also your Clapham Junction."

"That's right."

"You know there's a Clapham Junction here?"

"No. I didn't think there was a railway here?"

"Not any more. There was a railway once. It ran from here to Mdina. We called it, how do you say?" William looked at Violet but she shrugged, "ah yes the land ship but it ended when I was a young man, not much older than Daniel. Has Daniel taken you to Mdina?"

"No."

"Ah you must go to the silent city."

"Why is it called that?"

"Because all the rich and powerful that lived there would not let anyone speak," said William jovially.

"Is that true?" asked Jenny.

"I don't know but cars are banned so it's a quieter city," said Daniel.

"They have good architecture too. Norman and Baroque, which you like yes?" said William.

"Yes."

"So you will like it and also the cake. Very good cake you both will like," said William.

"Can we go?" asked Jenny.

"Of course," said William, "Daniel will take you. You catch the bus from here. Get off in Rabat and walk a little way to the city gates."

Jenny looked at Daniel.

"We'll go today," said Daniel

"That is good. You will like it."

"You never finished telling me about Clapham Junction," said Jenny.

"Oh I didn't?" said William delighted that he might spin another story.

"That's enough now," said Violet to William.

"But Vi she wants to know."

"Let them go and explore, make some of their own stories."

"Yes, yes. I walk with you and make sure you get on the right bus."

William got up to get his jacket and cap whilst Daniel went over to kiss his grandmother goodbye.

"We'll soon be heading home," said Daniel to his grandmother.

"Time passes too quickly," she said sadly. "One day we were young, the next like this."

"It's not too bad is it?" asked Daniel.

"No, we get old that is all."

"We'll see you again before we go."

"We will be here."

Daniel kissed and hugged his grandmother. Jenny did not escape without the same affectionate parting.

"Be happy together," Violet said to Jenny.

They followed William out of the flat and down the many flights of stairs. Daniel looked back and saw his grandmother watching them leave. She waved goodbye to them and they left the building. William talked to them all the way to the bus terminus where he put them on board the bus to Mdina. He waited for the bus to leave and waved them away. Daniel felt himself feeling sad and it showed.

"What's the matter?" asked Jenny.

"Sometimes I'm afraid that it will be the last time I see them."

"Don't think that," she said.

"I can't help it. It's the natural order of things."

"Perhaps but we have to hold onto the best moments or we'd do nothing but be afraid of the future."

"Sometimes it's difficult to remember the good things when you're afraid you're going to lose those you love."

"I know but you still have to hold on, no matter what,

okay?"

"Okay."

"Promise me that you'll hold on to the happier memories," said Jenny insistently.

"I promise."

"Now tell me the story behind Malta's Clapham Junction."

Daniel's sadness lifted and he wondered how his grandfather would have told the story but all he could do was tell her what little he knew.

"It's an ancient area where there are deep grooves in the ground called cart ruts. They are almost like car skid marks but cut down into the rock. No one knows how or why they are there but there are plenty of theories."

"Such as?"

"Everything from ancient paths, irrigation ditches to UFO landing strips."

"Maybe we can see them sometime too?"

"Well this bus goes to Dingli, and the cart ruts are, maybe, a half hour walk from there."

"I don't mind the walk."

"We won't have much time to see Rabat in the light but we could still get cake in Mdina."

"That sounds perfect."

They remained on the bus until it reached Dingli where they got off and walked parallel to the coast, south east to the Clapham Junction cart ruts. There they found the strange grooves, cut into the limestone in long straight parallels but some ruts were thin and deep, others shallow and wide. After an hour of looking around they left more baffled than before they arrived. They walked back into Dingli and took the bus through Rabat for the second time before getting off and walking through the gardens close to Mdina. From the garden they could see the fortified walls of the city and with the sun in descent in the sky they crossed the bridge and entered Mdina through the main city gate. It was as if they stepped back in time and the rest of the modern world was far behind them. The ancient buildings rose up above them from the fortified court yard. Each building around them was decorated ornately from small flourishes to carved statues. At first it was difficult to see where they could go from the court yard but Daniel led the way through the narrow streets passing massive wooden doors with intricately carved door knockers, iron decorated window cages and through arches and around corners. It was utterly confusing to all but those who knew their way. Daniel led Jenny with intent until they came to St. Paul's square at the end of which stood the baroque cathedral surrounded by elegant town houses all reflecting a diverse architectural style.

Daniel took Jenny inside the cathedral to view the stained glass windows and frescoes depicting saints and angels, the Corinthian pilasters, the chapels, the octagonal dome and the rich tessellated floor. It was a feast of dazzling riches created in worship of God. A divine power filled the cathedral and as they stood beneath the dome the setting sun's rays poured through the glass. The whole cathedral filled with the warm light and danced around them as it penetrated their very souls vanquishing all but the deepest of shadows. Daniel could feel Jenny holding his hand and everything felt right. It felt as if they had been given God's blessing. The sun light danced all around them and over them like a thousand angels. In that moment Daniel knew he wanted to marry Jenny and they stood basking in the power of belief, until the light diminished and the cool shadows began to return.

They both left the cathedral feeling changed and followed the street from the square to the edge of the fortified walls. As the sun was setting they looked from the walls out across the island as the lights started to flicker on. In the distance Daniel pointed out Mosta Dome, Sliema, Valletta and Luqa and then he took her to a small tea room for cake. As the sun continued to set they sat on the terrace gazing over the island and eating two large slices of chocolate gateaux. The heat of the day began to fade away but it did not bother either of them as they huddled closer to each other. Together they watched as the sun went down. It never failed to astound Daniel. A brilliant spectrum of colours erupted in the sky, with graduations of pinks, reds, yellows and oranges. They burned in the sky filling him with new confidence, hopes and dreams. He felt as if his life had been so confused before he met Jenny but now everything was clear. The veil of doubt and uncertainty had been lifted and with every passing moment the stronger his feelings grew. He had found something, someone, who made living worthwhile.

Daniel and Jenny remained in the city until the night had set in and so under lamplight they made their way from the city and out of the main gate. On the other side the darkness rushed in and enclosed them. All they could do was turn to look back upon the mighty silent city with its buildings a flaming torch of light and warmth. The pleasant daytime garden did little to comfort them in the darkness away from the radiating power of Mdina. With every step they took away from the city Daniel felt it calling them back. Tempting them to feel the immortality of history once more but it wasn't to history his attention was shifting it was the future. His future with Jenny. One he wanted to secure, to make as solid as the walls of the city, but as warm as the sun light that fell upon them every day.

As the bus moved further and further from Mdina they both looked back mile after mile at what once was the most powerful city in all of Malta until the city's lights were completely eclipsed.

"I'm glad your grandfather sent us," said Jenny.

"So am I," said Daniel.

"The cathedral was stunning."

"It really was," said Daniel as the memory returned to him of how much he wanted to spend the rest of his life with her.

"You've been quiet."

"I'm sorry. Things today kind of made me a little more reflective than usual."

"Anything I can help you with?"

"Yes but you would probably think I was crazy."

"You can try me."

Daniel seriously thought about proposing to her right at that moment but fear took hold of him and he thought better of it.

"Another time. I hope," he said.

"I hope so too."

Daniel put his arm around her and she rested her head on his shoulder. He breathed in her scent. That sweet smell of strawberries which made him hungry to taste her lips and he longed for the journey back to the hotel to be over with, so he could lie next to her once more. He whispered softly in Jenny's ear,

"I love you."

In his mind he added a few extra words, "and always

will."

When they arrived back at the hotel they went to Jenny's room.

"Do you mind if I take a shower?" asked Daniel.

"No, go ahead."

Daniel went into the bathroom and undressed. He tested the shower temperature and decided to keep it a little cooler in the hope it would help him think. As he showered he could not stop thinking about Jenny and how he was so close to everything he had ever desired. The very thought of her gave him butterflies in his stomach. The voice in his mind told him exactly what he wanted to do but there was another voice telling him that it was too soon and he didn't know which one to listen to. There were so many reasons and excuses not to ask Jenny to marry him and it seemed only one reason to ask her, because he loved her. The cool water wasn't helping him at all and so he increased the temperature, hoping that might relax him. There was a knock on the door and Jenny stepped inside,

"Do you mind if I join you?" she asked.

"No, go ahead," he said repeating her words.

## Chapter Ten

When Jenny awoke it was with the knowledge that they only had a couple of days left together. As they made their way towards Marsa she tried to imagine what it would be like without Daniel. Even though they had only been together for such a short time she found it difficult to think about her life without him. The whole time they had been together Jenny had never ceased to be surprised. That morning she had found flowers from him waiting for her. When he had done it she did not know but it made her morning all the better. His note had made her smile all the more. The simplest of words that reassured her and dispelled all of her pain and troubles. Such was the power of her feelings that she felt blinded to anything else. She had felt that from the moment they met and she found it inexplicable.

As they passed through Marsa Jenny saw a power station and for a moment thought about the boat tour she had taken with Sarah and Lisa. She felt a twinge of guilt for having left them again with little but a note promising to see them that afternoon but then Daniel was doing the same with his brother and Matthew. That thought did not make her feel much better.

"Am I keeping you from your family?" she asked.

"No. What made you think that?"

"I was thinking about Sarah and Lisa and then about you and your brother."

"It's okay."

"What about your family here?"

"We don't get to see them as much as I'd like but they all have their own lives, their own families."

"But you are a part of their family too."

"I know and we find ways to spend time together."

"So am I stopping you from doing that?"

"No of course not."

"I don't want to come between you and your family."

"You aren't."

"But you don't get over here all that often do you?"

"Not as much as we used to."

"You must miss them."

"I do, but as I said everyone lives their own lives."

"Do they visit you in England?"

"They have done but less and less frequently."

"So maybe you should spend more time with them whilst you're here?"

"Is there something you aren't telling me?"

"What do you mean?"

"It sounds like, maybe, you want me to give you some space?"

"No. I didn't want you to think that. I was feeling guilty for all the time we've spent together, and I don't want you to resent me for it."

"I don't resent you. It's really not an issue and I think this is our stop," said Daniel ringing the bell.

They got off the bus in an area that was a mixture of the traditional limestone residential buildings surrounded by a growing industrial zone. Jenny was not certain where they were going but she had seen signs for a winery, a correctional facility, several sports clubs and now they were surrounded by small shops. She looked at Daniel and saw that he had taken out a map from his bag and was unfolding it.

"This is different," said Jenny.

"Well I like to keep things interesting."

"That you do."

"And I don't quite know how to get to our next stop."

"Well now I'm even more intrigued."

"Sometimes a map makes things easier," said Daniel leading the way.

"So where are we going?"

Daniel took a piece of paper from his pocket and handed it to her. She read it and saw that it was from Rocco.

"Hal Saflieni Hypogeum?" she said quite uncertain of any of the pronunciation.

"The hypogeum," said Daniel.

It only took them a couple of minutes until they reached the unassuming entrance and Jenny was quite uncertain of what they were going to find. However one thing that she did notice was that it said it was closed for restoration. They went inside and Jenny could see the signs for a small museum that appeared to be under construction.

"I don't think we should be in here," said Jenny.

"You might be right," said Daniel.

A man approached them and Jenny felt herself fill with apprehension that they were about to be told off.

"Hello, are you Rocco's nephew?"

"Yes, I'm Daniel."

"And Jenny, right?" said the man.

"Yes," said Jenny.

"I'm Paul, your uncle gave me a call and said you'd been to the temples."

"We went to Ħaġar Qim," said Daniel.

"They are beautiful, hopefully we'll get to protect them too one day."

"Is that what's happening here?" asked Jenny.

"Yes. We're restoring and conserving the temple so we're closed to the public. But we can make one or two exceptions."

Jenny still did not know what she was going to see but she felt uniquely privileged as they followed Paul down into the hypogeum. The rooms were like caves, some natural, some carved out with details and refinement that she had not expected especially from an incredibly ancient society, dating back over five thousand years.

"So this is the first level," said Paul, "it's quite similar to the tombs found in Xemsija. Where it gets more exciting is on the second level."

Daniel and Jenny followed him down to the next level where it was separated into several rooms.

"This is the Main Chamber. This is where they found the sleeping lady which is in the National Museum."

"What is the sleeping lady?" asked Jenny.

"One of several statues that was originally found here, some call them goddesses or mother figures but that's beyond my area of expertise."

"How long is the restoration going to take?" asked Daniel.

"Best guess the better part of ten years."

"Wow," said Daniel.

"It has to be done. People were roaming around, unaccompanied causing all kinds of damage and if it hadn't been closed when it was I think we'd have lost it forever."

"That would have been terrible," said Jenny.

"Yes. But we're hoping to fit walkways," said Paul showing them the work in progress, "along with climate and lighting control to protect the ochre here in the Oracle Room."

They followed Paul as he pointed out what resembled cave paintings in red ochre in the small rectangular chamber.

"It's incredible," said Jenny.

"I'm afraid I can't show you much more because of the work we're doing but you can glimpse another room through there."

Daniel and Jenny peered to see the circular room with inward slanting walls decorated with geometric patterns of spirals.

"There's a third level as well," said Paul.

They followed him down to view the third level before he led them back up and showed them the Holy of Holies chamber. Jenny looked at the chamber with the stacked triliths.

"The trilithons are impressive" said Jenny.

"They are. The ceiling here also might indicate how the surface temples were covered."

"What are trilithons?" asked Daniel.

"Two vertical stones supporting a horizontal stone,"

said Jenny.

Daniel nodded.

"Like Stonehenge," said Jenny echoing Sarah's words from the temple they had visited.

"And they're both World Heritage Sites," said Paul.

"It really is amazing," said Jenny. "I never would have thought any of this was here."

"Well I'm glad I could show it you," said Paul.

Jenny tried to absorb every detail of the temple as they followed Paul back to the main entrance but it felt beyond her comprehension how or why any of it existed. Whilst she could understand the engineering behind it, seeing it made it feel unreal.

"Thank you," Jenny and Daniel said to Paul.

"You're welcome. Always happy to do a favour for Rocco."

Jenny waved goodbye and they left through the same unassuming entranceway they had come in by.

"Didn't you think that was amazing?" asked Jenny.

"It was," said Daniel. "I've never been there before."

"So it was your first time?"

"Yes."

"Thank you," said Jenny kissing him and then looking back at the outside of the Hypogeum.

"You'd never know it was there. Would you?" said Daniel.

"No. It's almost completely hidden away," said Jenny.

"I guess we should make our way back."

"Do you know the way?"

"I think so."

They walked for a short while until they came upon a sign for a winery. Jenny remembered she had seen signs for it on their way to the Hypogeum.

"Do you mind if we go in?" she asked.

Daniel shook his head and so they entered the winery through the shop where they were greeted by an older lady.

"Welcome," she said. "Are you here for the tour?"

"Actually I was looking for a bottle of wine for Daniel's uncle," said Jenny.

"Well we can certainly do that," said the lady.

"To thank him," Jenny said to Daniel.

"Please come over. Let me pour you some samples and I'm sure we will find the perfect wine for your uncle."

She poured them several glasses and asked,

"Do you know what type of wine your uncle likes?"

"Not really," said Daniel, "but he's a local."

"Ah, well in that case you cannot go wrong with one of our new wines from Marnisi in Marsaxlokk. It is a red of very noble character. It is very enjoyable."

Daniel and Jenny both tasted the wine and that was enough to convince them. Daniel started to get out his wallet but Jenny stopped him.

"Let me buy it for him" said Jenny.

"You don't have to do that."

"I want to. Everyone has been so nice and we should get something for your grandparents too."

"Well if you're sure?"

"I am."

"Then we'll split the bill okay?"

"Okay."

They bought the wine and left the shop.

"Shall we head towards Valletta? It'll be easier to catch a bus back to Sliema from there." said Daniel.

"Lead the way."

They headed back towards Valletta and then onwards to Sliema. On approaching the hotel Jenny saw Lisa and Sarah sunbathing at the hotel's outdoor pool and so they went over to them. Sarah was the first to see them and nudged Lisa from her semi meditative state.

"Hi girls," said Jenny.

"Well look who's here," said Lisa. "I guess you must have had a very good day yesterday?"

Her tone was salacious but Jenny did not bite.

"We did, thank you," said Jenny.

"I'm glad," said Lisa. "Why don't you tell us all about it?"

"We visited Daniel's grandparents, and then we saw some cart tracks and the cathedral in Mdina."

"Oh," said Lisa disappointedly, "and?"

"And we had a lovely time," said Jenny.

"I was hoping for something a little more-" said Lisa before being cut off.

"Leave her be," said Sarah.

"Well did you have a good time?" Lisa asked Daniel still searching for a few more scintillating details.

"Yes, we both did. It was very interesting."

"Fine," said Lisa.

"Do you know where Phillip and Matthew are?" asked Daniel.

Lisa shrugged.

"We haven't seen them today," said Sarah.

"Maybe you should go and find them?" said Lisa.

"It's okay," said Jenny. "You should go and check on them,"

"I'll be right back."

"There's no hurry," said Lisa.

Sarah nudged Lisa but it did not change her tone.

Instead she watched as Daniel went back towards the hotel and disappeared from sight.

"Now come on tell us everything," said Lisa.

"There's nothing to tell," said Jenny.

"We didn't make sure you had the day to yourselves for nothing. We want details. Intimate details."

"I'm not going to tell you about that."

"And she doesn't have to," said Sarah.

"You know I'd tell you," said Lisa.

"That's why we don't ask," said Sarah.

"Well if you won't spill the juicy parts then at least tell me everything is okay."

"It is," said Jenny.

"And you still have feelings?"

"We do."

Lisa pretended to shake off the idea of feelings.

"So have you figured out what happens next?" asked Sarah.

"No."

"Love them and leave them I say," said Lisa.

"You mean screw them and leave them," said Sarah.

"What's the difference?" asked Lisa.

"You'll find out one day," said Sarah.

"I doubt it," said Lisa looking at Jenny.

"I hope you're wrong," said Jenny. "I hope you both find love."

Lisa's reaction to the idea was clear. She too often mistook the physical for the emotional and was having a hard time dealing with the fall out of her latest fling with Phillip. Sarah's reaction on the other hand was almost unperceivable but Jenny knew she wanted to feel love and so she sat down next to her and gave her a hug.

"It will happen for you too one day," said Jenny.

"I hope so," said Sarah

"It will."

"Then you'll both have to be bridesmaids."

"We will, won't we Lisa?"

"I hope so," said Lisa.

"Ignore her," said Sarah, "she's still grouchy."

"Why?" asked Jenny.

"Because," said Lisa.

"She's still hung up on Phillip," said Sarah.

"Are you?" asked Jenny.

"No."

"Are you sure?"

"Yes."

"I'm not sure I believe you," said Jenny.

Lisa sighed deeply and said,

"I wish they felt as bad afterwards."

"After breaking up?"

"Yes."

"Did something happen yesterday?" asked Jenny.

"No and that's the point. He carried on as if nothing had ever happened between us."

"How did you want him to act?"

"I wanted him to be upset or to hit on me or something. Maybe even to look at me like Daniel looks at you."

Jenny felt upset for her friend but did not know what she could do. It was a pattern that she feared Lisa would have to break on her own. As for how Daniel looked at her? She had thought that it was only in her own mind that she saw his love for her. They remained by the pool trying to support Lisa until Daniel returned. Jenny was glad he came back alone for Lisa's sake. She also felt that she could not leave her friends again so soon and so the four of them went for lunch.

# CHAPTER ELEVEN

Daniel was quite silent during lunch with Jenny and her friends. He sat and listened to them but mostly he watched Jenny. He liked watching her interact with her friends, it showed another side to her that he found fascinating. It was a glimpse into a perspective he had never really seen growing up with a brother. At times it seemed that there was little structure to their conversation, it seemed random, populated with tangents of popular culture and idle daydreams. Occasionally Jenny or Sarah would try to engage him in the conversation but his own responses didn't seem to trigger any particular further discussion and so he began to hope that somehow he might extradite Jenny. It was difficult for him to talk to them without having the same shared experiences or at least the same frames of reference. It made him feel quite lost with only Jenny as his anchor. Without her he would be completely lost. The point was brought home clearly when Jenny stepped away from the table for a couple of minutes and instantly he felt completely closed out of the group.

He tried to imagine what it would have been like if he had been sat there before he had met Jenny but he could not imagine a scenario without her. For without her he had been incomplete and only when they were together did anything make sense. That was when he felt afraid. Afraid of a life without her, that she would leave him and find someone else. The thought crystallised his mind. He had to make sure they could never be parted. To tell her that she was the only one for him now and forever. When she returned to the table he felt a surge of panic. He wanted her to stay with him so much and the voice in his mind told him that his future only existed with her. It was a strange feeling, to know absolutely that something had to be. Stranger still to have to walk away from the person he was destined to be with but in that moment he felt anxiety welling up within him. All he could do was excuse himself and hope that he could find a way to settle his nerves.

In his confused state Daniel wished he knew where Phillip and Matthew were. He longed for someone to talk to even though the person he really wanted to talk to was only a few metres from him. He went to the bar, hoping that Jenny had not seen his panic, that she did not think he was running from her. Daniel never wanted her to see him so weak and confused. Neither did he want her to see him an insane person and surely, he thought to himself, that would be exactly what she thought it he asked her to marry him. He ordered whiskey, neat, and drank it swiftly. It burned his throat before he felt it warming his core. For a moment he thought about ordering another one but he did not want Jenny to think he was a drunkard either. Further it was not doing anything to settle his nerves and so he sat at the bar and watched her until she came over to him.

"You're safe now," said Jenny.

He didn't know what to say.

"Come on," said Jenny taking his hand. "It's time for a siesta."

Daniel followed Jenny back to her room and to her bed where she pushed him down and straddled him.

"You know the idea of a siesta is to rest," said Daniel.

"You can rest," said Jenny pulling off his shirt.

He looked at her and relaxed as she ran her hands over his chest. She bent over and kissed him and then sat upright and Daniel could see that she was thinking about something else.

"What are you thinking about?" he asked.

"How strange life is."

"Good strange or bad?"

"Both I guess."

"And is this good?"

She bent down again and kissed him tenderly.

"Definitely good."

"And the bad?"

Daniel could see Jenny working through her thoughts, reflecting on something and all he could do was wait for her to speak again.

"I wish nothing had happened between your brother and Lisa."

"I know," said Daniel feeling the same. "He doesn't feel all that great about how things went either."

"How do you know?"

"He kind of said."

"Lisa doesn't think he cares at all."

"He does. I think."

"Are you sure?"

"Not exactly."

"So it was just a fling and now he's done with her?"

"He said he wanted more."

"With Lisa?"

Daniel thought back to what Phillip had said and Jenny took his silence as a no.

"So he doesn't care about her?" asked Jenny.

"It's different. He's different."

"From you?"

"Yes."

"So I'm not just a fling for you?"

"No you're not."

"You don't want to discard me like he did her?"

"No I don't and I thought they were going to be friends?"

"Isn't that always a lie?"

"Maybe."

"You know she's hurting."

"I think he is too."

"Is he really?"

"He wants something he hasn't found."

"So does she."

"But I don't think he knows what it is."

"Do you?"

"I know that I want you."

"Do you now."

"Yes."

"You don't want to be friends?"

"I thought we already were."

"Just friends?" teased Jenny.

"You'll always be more than that to me. I wish I could

find a way to show you how much I love you."

"Maybe you can."

Daniel struggled to sit up and kiss her. She let him but then pushed him back down.

"Relax," she said running her hand down to his lower abdomen.

It was early evening when they emerged from their afternoon siesta to take a walk away from the hotel, around Tigné Point, until they found a quiet area of the rocky beach. They walked over the smooth flat rocks towards the sea. Removing her shoes Jenny paddled in the surf holding Daniel's hand to avoid slipping. He looked as her feet pushed through the water and the spray from the waves splashed her legs. She slipped a little and pulled on his hand to keep her balance. He held onto her tightly. It felt perfect to him. Their being together. Her hand in his. Her left hand. He looked at her ring finger and imagined what it might be like to propose to her, to slip the ring over her finger. Daniel imagined how surprised she would be and how happy. How with one word, yes, their lives would change forever. They would never have to be apart or feel lonely again. Could he? Could he really propose? There was only one reason not too – it was too soon. Daniel wondered if that was enough of a reason not to ask but he was not sure. He knew his own mind and that he loved her completely. Her love made him feel a warm and radiant pulse spread through his whole body. He asked himself if it was a bigger risk to ask too soon or too late. Could there be a too late? As he watched Jenny paddling through the gently lapping waves he tried to push such thoughts to the back of his mind so he could enjoy being with her in the present. He took off his shoes and walked in the water next to her, both holding onto each other for support on the slippery rocks.

Even though he had tried to suppress his thoughts they kept resurfacing as they walked back to the hotel and as they sat together for their evening meal. Daniel wanted to talk to Jenny to see if he could find a clue as to how she might react but talking about the future also meant accepting that their time together was coming to an end. That in two days she would be at the airport. The thought of it made him nervous. He did not want to lose her because they lived in different places, because they had different lives or because normal life made their being together impossible. It seemed there was no simple way to answer his questions. They left the restaurant and looked into the hotel bar where they saw Matthew sitting alone. Daniel and Jenny went over to him.

"Good evening," said Daniel.

"Oh hello," said Matthew pleased to see someone else. "Are you on your own?"

"Yes."

"Where's Phillip?"

"I don't know. I came down for breakfast and he was sleeping but when I went back he was gone."

"I'm sorry," said Daniel, "I thought he was with you."

"It's okay."

"No it's not," said Jenny. "I'm sorry. I've been keeping Daniel to myself."

"I don't mind. I mean you two are... well you're together," said Matthew.

"Now I feel even worse," said Jenny looking at Matthew sat alone.

"So do I," said Daniel sitting down with Jenny opposite Matthew.

"Have you been on your own all day?" asked Jenny.

"Yes."

"If we'd known you could have come with us," said Jenny.

"I don't mind having a little quiet time."

"I really hope I haven't ruined your holiday."

"Not at all and I've never seen Daniel so happy."

Daniel felt a little awkward but he knew Matthew was right.

"Truly?" asked Jenny.

"Yes. You two are really good together. It's nice to see."

"Thank you."

"I wish I could say the same about Phillip and your friend."

"I know. I think she's regretting it."

"When we were with them yesterday I could feel the tension between them. I hope that whatever it is you won't let it affect you and Daniel?"

"It won't. I know Lisa's hurt but she knows it was by her own actions as well as his."

"It's too bad really."

"Yes it is."

"I hope it isn't going to make things awkward," said Daniel.

"What do you mean?" asked Jenny.

"This thing between Phillip and Lisa."

"It's only awkward for them."

"Only for a couple more days though," said Matthew.

The reminder of how little time they had left together made Daniel and Jenny look at each other with uncertainty and a little sadness.

"You'll work it out," said Matthew.

"Yes we will," said Daniel.

"I hope so," said Jenny.

"It's not so difficult. You exchange details, you write, you call, you visit," said Matthew.

"Of course," said Daniel thinking that was the more sensible approach than his grandiose ideas.

"Did I say something wrong?" asked Matthew looking at Daniel and then Jenny.

"No, not at all," she said. "We just need to talk about it."

"And we will but not tonight. Tonight we're at your disposal," Daniel said to Matthew.

"Yes we are so what would you like to do?" asked Jenny.

"Well I wouldn't mind a change of scenery, maybe one of the local bars?"

"We can do that can't we?" Daniel asked Jenny.

"Yes of course."

"And the first few rounds are on me," said Daniel.

Daniel took Jenny's hand and together with Matthew they left the hotel and headed towards a strip of bars and pubs. The first bar they entered was busy and it took them a while to be served. It was standing room only and the music was too loud forcing them to shout to try and be heard.

"It's loud in here," said Matthew.

"What?" said Daniel unable to hear him.

"It's too loud."

"Yeah."

Daniel still could not really hear him. All they could do was stand and drink and they might as well have been doing that alone. The level of the music made it uncomfortable, Daniel could feel it straining his eardrums. He found himself taking longer and more frequent drinks to try and be done quicker. He looked at Matthew and Jenny. They looked like rigid machines only able to perform one task, limited by the structures imposed on them.

"Are you okay?" Daniel asked Jenny loudly.

She could not hear him at all and pointed to her ear and shook her head. They were penned in, hardly able to move and completely unable to talk to each other which made Daniel decide it was pointless being there and so he gestured towards the exit. Jenny nodded and Matthew quickly finished his drink so they could all leave. When they emerged from the building it was as if they had been cut free from their restraints and they could move and talk normally once more. They walked along the street a little way looking in on several bars that appeared equally as busy until they saw what looked like a small place without too many people. They decided to give it a try and went inside. From the outside it had looked very narrow but inside they saw that the building and bar went a long way back. Matching the length of the bar was a wall of bottles of every kind of alcoholic beverage they could imagine. Nearly all the seating was along the bar except for a couple of booths at the far end which were already taken. The three of them sat at the bar and tried to take in some of the wide array of beverages. They ordered what they knew and settled back in their seats for a more leisurely time.

"This is a bit more like it," said Matthew.

"I have to agree," said Daniel.

"I suspect Lisa might have preferred the crowds but this suits me," said Jenny.

"So we can relax a while, talk, drink, be merry," said Daniel.

"Not too merry," said Jenny.

"No midnight swimming," said Matthew.

"You won't get any arguments from me on that one," said Daniel.

"I wonder how long it would take to try one of each drink?" asked Matthew.

"I couldn't imagine," said Jenny.

"I don't know but I hope you wouldn't try and do it all in one sitting," said Daniel.

"I think this will do me for the night. Though it is good to be out from the hotel," said Matthew.

"It's been okay so far, hasn't it?"

"Yes it has. It's always good to take a break with old and new friends," said Matthew offering a little toast to Jenny.

They chinked their glasses together and sipped a little. It made Daniel happy to know that Matthew could view Jenny as a friend. Especially when she meant so much more to him.

"Hopefully Lisa and Phillip can set aside things for a couple more days," said Matthew.

"Or avoid each other," said Daniel.

"That might be better," added Jenny.

"Either way so long as we can enjoy the time we have left," said Matthew, "and you can both work out what happens next I'm sure."

"We will," said Jenny.

Her words gave Daniel a good feeling about the future and let him think about other things for a while. His thoughts turned to his brother and where he might be.

"If that's okay?" she asked.

"Yes of course. I was wondering about Phillip."

"I'm sure he's okay," said Matthew.

"I'm sure he is too," said Jenny.

"Ah, he's fine," said Daniel, "it's not uncommon for him to go off by himself on a whim."

"That's true but it usually leads to some kind of trouble," said Matthew.

"Should we try and find him?" asked Jenny.

"He or someone will call if he gets into any real trouble," said Daniel.

"Are you sure?"

"We'll probably find him fast asleep in bed by the time we get back."

"That wouldn't surprise me either," said Matthew.

"So he does this kind of thing a lot?" asked Jenny.

"He gets itchy feet," said Matthew.

"The wanderlust," added Daniel.

"I see. Is that inherited?" asked Jenny.

"I don't think so."

"So you won't want to leave me on a whim?"

Daniel could not quite tell if she was serious or teasing him, but his answer was always going to be the same.

"I never want to leave you."

She smiled and he asked himself if she knew how much of a spell she had cast over him. They lingered in the bar for a while after they finished drinking, enjoying the atmosphere and fascinated by the array of beverages until the conversation seemed played out and they felt it was time to return to the hotel where, almost as predicted, Daniel and Matthew found Phillip asleep in their room. Content in the knowledge that his brother was safe and well he bid Matthew goodnight but at the doorway he paused.

"Do you really like Jenny?" Daniel asked Matthew.

"Yes, very much so."

"When you said we should talk, write or visit in the future. Well I know you're right..."

"But?"

"I don't want to lose her."

"I don't think you will. She's clearly fallen for you as much as you have for her."

"How can you be sure?"

"It's in the way she looks at you. The way you are together."

"Would you think I was crazy if I told you I wanted more?"

"More than what?"

"More than writing and visits."

"That will come with time."

"What if I wanted to make certain that it did?"

"I don't know how you could do that. Do you?"

"No I guess not. I'm thinking out loud. That's all."

"Take it a step at a time, talk to each other and you'll get there."

"You're right. Thanks."

"You're welcome. Now go and be happy together okay?"

"Okay. You know if you want to do something tomorrow we can."

"Let's wait and see what tomorrow brings. Now go before she comes to her senses and locks you out."

"Good night."

"Good night."

As Daniel left he heard Matthew shut the door behind him and in the brief moments between his room and hers he thought about nothing other than how he could secure a future with Jenny. More and more he felt himself wanting to throw caution and logic away. He wanted to make a leap because to do anything else felt as if it would be wasting time. Time that they could be together, building their lives and their futures.

## Chapter Twelve

Phillip's absence seemed to be becoming a theme as the group sat down for breakfast together.

"No Phillip?" Daniel asked Matthew.

"He didn't seem to want to get up."

"Is that the polite version?"

"Yes."

"Well maybe I'll try waking him later."

"Rather you than me."

"Is there anything you want to do today?"

"It depends on everyone else."

Jenny was glad that Matthew had been so understanding of how much time she and Daniel had spent together. She was also slightly relieved that Lisa and Phillip were effectively being kept separate from each other. Matthew was still waiting to hear about the day's plans and it was Lisa who took the lead.

"Well I've planned a girl's day for us," she said.

"You did?" asked Sarah.

"Yes."

"What is it?" asked Jenny.

"I booked a whole day for us at the spa and salon."

Jenny was rather bewildered by Lisa's sudden action and she looked at Daniel knowing that a spa day meant spending her last full day without him.

"Don't look so sad," said Lisa. "You can spend all night together."

"I know, but we're leaving tomorrow."

"She's right," said Sarah, "which is why you should spend the day relaxing."

"We've hardly been overdoing it. Have we?" said Jenny looking at Daniel for support.

"Well, I didn't think so but maybe a spa day could be good?" he said uncertainly.

"It will," said Lisa, "and no is not an answer."

"It is," said Jenny, "but not one you want to hear."

Lisa shrugged but Jenny knew she was going with them even though she did not want to be parted from Daniel. She had been willing to share him. That much she had accepted yesterday when they were talking with Matthew but she did not want to be without him. As they continued to eat breakfast together all she could do was listen as Daniel and Matthew began to make their own plans for the day. At times Daniel would look at her and even though he did not say anything in front of the others she knew he had wanted to be with her too. Once they had finished breakfast they took a moment to speak privately.

"I really did want to spend the day with you," said Jenny.

"I know. I wanted to be with you too but I'm sure you'll

enjoy the spa and maybe I could take you somewhere special this evening?"

"What did you have in mind?"

"Something romantic."

"That sounds intriguing."

"I'll meet you back here at around six?"

"I can't wait."

As they began to part Jenny still felt a little sad about leaving him.

"Don't be upset with your friends," said Daniel.

"I'm not but I feel like we don't have much time."

"We'll find a way to make things work."

"I hope so."

"We will," said Daniel.

They kissed and parted with Jenny leaving with Sarah and Lisa to get ready for the spa whilst Daniel stayed behind with Matthew.

"I've never seen anyone so sad about going to the spa," said Lisa.

"I'm not sad about that," said Jenny.

"She's teasing you," said Sarah.

"We're all going to have fun," said Lisa.

"Not everyone enjoys the same things."

"No but I'm going to enjoy this. The masseur looks hot."

"I'm sure he does."

Sarah and Jenny both rolled their eyes and knew all they could do was to go along with her.

At the spa Lisa was keen to start with the jacuzzi and her massage session but Jenny and Sarah both opted out. They were reunited at lunch which they weren't surprised to find was spa food that would have struggled to satisfy a rabbit.

"How was the masseur?" asked Jenny.

"He was sweet," said Lisa.

"Did you get his number?" asked Sarah.

"No but I gave him mine."

"I bet you did," said Sarah.

Lisa only answered with an expression that did not confirm or deny either of their suspicions.

"Well I'm glad you enjoyed yourself," said Jenny.

"Hey, come on you're having fun aren't you?" asked Lisa.

"Yes we are," said Jenny.

"See I knew this is what we needed."

"We needed?" asked Sarah.

"Maybe I needed it but it's not just about me," said Lisa.

"We know," said Sarah.

"I wanted to do something nice for you," Lisa said to Jenny.

"You have," replied Jenny.

"Beyond the miniature lunch portion it's been good," said Sarah.

"Isn't that what spa days are all about? Overpriced treatments, tiny lunches, hot men," said Lisa.

"And spending time together," said Jenny looking at them both.

"We don't need a spa and beauty session to do that though do we?" asked Sarah.

"Not really," said Lisa.

"So why else did we come here?" Sarah asked Lisa.

"Well I thought that bit might have been kind of obvious," said Lisa.

"It is?" asked Sarah.

"I think so," said Jenny.

"Did I miss something?"

"It's all about him isn't it?" asked Jenny.

"Him who?" asked Sarah.

"The one that got away, or the one that broke up with us or said let's just be friends."

"Oh I see," said Sarah, "so this is all about Phillip."

"And the rest," said Lisa.

"Wasn't it your choice to be friends?"

"It was," said Lisa, "but I want to make sure he knows what he's missing out on."

"You can be quite wicked at times," said Sarah.

"Maybe," said Lisa. "Consider it a reminder. I want to walk back in the hotel and break his heart with a single look."

"Lisa, that's so mean," said Jenny.

"I'm going to make sure you do the same to Daniel too," said Lisa.

"I don't want to break his heart," said Jenny.

"You don't have to but you have to remind him how lucky he is to have you."

"He knows."

"After tonight he'll never stop appreciating you."

"Maybe you're not so wicked after all," said Sarah.

"Don't believe it," said Lisa getting up and brazenly fetching several more lunches.

At six o'clock that evening Lisa's heartbreaker hypothesis was put to the test when the three girls entered the hotel lobby. Jenny could not believe how nervous she felt. Her hair was up, and set in place with so many bobby pins she could feel the weight of them. The dress made her even more self-conscious. It was very tight and bright red. Then there were her heels that seemed higher than ever. She looked at her friends who were watching her but also staring at Daniel, Phillip and Matthew awaiting their reaction. They weren't the only ones to react. The people in the lobby parted allowing Jenny to pass as she walked towards Daniel. There were several lingering gazes amongst the spectators and the disturbance gained Daniel's attention. He looked up and slowly rose to his feet and said,

"You look stunning."

"Thank you."

Jenny felt herself smile, not only because of the effect she could feel herself exuding on Daniel but because she was happy to be with him once more.

"Are you ready?" asked Daniel.

"Yes," said Jenny.

Daniel extended his arm and Jenny linked her arm with his.

"Where are we going?" she asked.

"Somewhere special."

Jenny looked back and saw that Phillip appeared quite distracted by Lisa which she hoped gave her the satisfaction she was looking for. Daniel led Jenny across to the bay and to a water taxi which took them from Sliema to Valletta. Jenny became acutely aware that Daniel was staring at her. She smiled at him and looked away at the water and the approaching city wondering what he was thinking about. The taxi took less than ten minutes to deliver them right into Valletta and it was a short walk from there to the restaurant.

They entered the restaurant where Daniel confirmed the reservation at the reception desk.

"Did you arrange all this today?" she asked.

"Yes," said Daniel.

"You have been busy."

They followed the host over to a table for two which had tall red candles along with a crystal bowl centre piece with floating candles all alight. Daniel pulled the chair out for Jenny and she sat down. The host handed them both the menu and said that their waiter would be with them shortly. Jenny glanced around the restaurant which was full. The interior was simple with light cream coloured walls and several paintings arranged neatly. She tried to see what some of the other patrons were eating before she looked over the menu and was glad to find English descriptions underneath some of the more exotic names like Stuffat Tal-Qarnit which was described as octopus stew. Another item was Bebbux bil-Faqqiegh which was snails and mushrooms and there was a soup called Soppa tal-Armla which was translated as Widow Soup consisting of vegetables and goat's cheese with an egg. The name made her shudder especially when every time she looked at Daniel she felt her heart racing faster and faster. She did not want it to stop. It was easy to imagine themselves years in the future repeating the same kind of evening. The thought of being torn apart, even many years ahead, was unbearable. When the waiter came over they ordered, starting with a Meze Malti, a selection of Maltese nibbles, which they could both share. For the main course Jenny was glad Daniel picked lamb over horse but she couldn't face either and so opted for Pixxispad, a swordfish dish. The waiter left and came back quickly with the drinks before departing once more.

"You look very beautiful," said Daniel.

"I like how you look too."

"But I'm not going to break anyone's heart and I think you might."

"Not yours though."

"I hope not."

"I don't want to."

She looked into his eyes and watched the flames from the candles dance there. Jenny wanted to hear Daniel tell her that he loved her one more time, for him to whisper it to her before he kissed her.

"What are you thinking?" asked Daniel.

"I'm thinking about you."

"I was thinking about you all day too."

"What did you do without me?"

"I woke Phillip up."

"Was it dangerous?"

"A little."

"But you survived."

"I did."

"Then what?"

"I tried to do some things I thought Matthew would enjoy."

"Were you successful?"

"I think so. We went to the Malta Experience. It's a cinematic history of the islands."

"That sounds good."

"What about your day?"

"Probably everything you imagine a spa day to be."

"So lots of attractive masseuses."

"Something like that."

"And lots of talk about men."

"A little."

"Should I be worried?"

"No, you shouldn't."

"Someone else should?"

Jenny thought about Lisa wanting to make Phillip see what he was missing out on and thought she'd probably done enough.

"I think we're all okay now," she said.

"What about in the future?" asked Daniel.

"I guess that is the question. Isn't it?"

She looked at Daniel and saw something in his expression.

"It is the question isn't it?" she asked again.

"Yes. It is."

He seemed lost in thought but Jenny was not sure if it was about the future or something else.

"So what are we going to do?"

"I want to keep seeing you."

"I want that to but it won't be simple."

"Maybe not."

"There is something I haven't been able to tell you. I haven't wanted to."

"I know."

"It never feels like the right time."

The setting was so romantic and the last thing Jenny wanted was to ruin the moment or their upcoming last day together but she was afraid that not talking about it would ultimately make it worse. Fear filled her mind and she thought that anything she said now could end their relationship.

"We do keep avoiding talking about it don't we," said Daniel.

"Yes."

Daniel leaned over the table and kissed her.

"And you keep doing that," said Jenny, "which makes it so much harder."

"I love you."

"And that makes it almost impossible."

"So what do we do?"

The waiter returned with their first course. Jenny looked at the food that they were being served. A selection of cheeses, sausages, stuffed olives, dried tomatoes and Maltese biscuits. She thought back over everything and she knew she could not carry on as they were.

"I can't do this to you," said Jenny.

"Do what?"

"Let you love me when I know I'm going to hurt you," she got up and began to leave. "I'm so sorry."

Daniel caught her arm.

"Don't leave."

"I have to."

The waiter looked at them both.

"Please," said Jenny tears forming in her eyes, "let me go."

"I can't."

Her reality became heightened and she could sense everyone looking at her, feel Daniel holding her arm, smell the scents of the food and feel her own heart breaking. Time seemed to slow and all she wanted to do was run.

## CHAPTER THIRTEEN

Jenny walked from the restaurant as quickly as she could and as soon as she was outside she took off her high heels and ran. She ran over the cobbled pavement, through deserted side streets until she came to the edge of the city where she slumped against the ancient fortified wall. Her heart was torn apart and she hated herself because she was the one who had done it. She wished none of it had ever happened, that she hadn't let herself fall in love. She blamed herself entirely and knew she had ruined everything. Jenny could still see Daniel's face as she left. He looked so confused, sad, lost and shocked. He deserved an explanation but she could not face him. She felt like she would never be able to face him again. Her whole body ached with agonising pain. Daniel was out of her life and she could never see him again. It was her fault. After everything they had seen, all they had experienced, the love they shared it had to end in misery. That was what life had determined for her she told herself. It was the way it had to be. She tried to calm down, take deep breaths of air, but her breathing was erratic, her mind confused. Jenny sat on the floor her dress torn from running, her feet blackened by the street and she cried until she could not cry any more.

Slowly Jenny stood up. She didn't know where she was and so had to walk through the streets hoping she would find somewhere she recognised. As Jenny was walking she felt terribly alone and vulnerable. There did not seem to be anyone else around. She kept walking and then she heard footsteps behind her. The narrow street was dimly lit and she felt afraid. She thought she deserved to be in her current predicament but it still terrified her. Jenny glanced behind her and saw an old man crossing the street and going down another one. She felt relieved that it had been nothing but her mind turned back to Daniel and how she had left him. She wanted to tell him how sorry she was but at the same time she knew she couldn't. Finally she found the main high street and there were lots more people. She passed a group of men sitting in the street all dressed in jeans and old shirts. They looked at her and it made her uncomfortable. She tried to straighten her dress. They said something to her in Maltese. Jenny carried on walking not understanding a word of it and hoped she was not making another mistake. The man who had spoken stood up and followed her. Jenny felt the man's hand on her shoulder. She turned around filled with apprehension. The man's face was dark from years of prolonged sun exposure. His hands were rough and his face dishevelled. He spoke to her in Maltese again. Jenny tried not to start crying.

"I don't understand," she said trying to sound as calm

as possible.

"Ah, you're a tourist," said the man.

Jenny nodded still uncertain what his intentions were.

"You are in trouble?" he asked.

Jenny could not answer she was afraid if she said anything she would start crying again.

"You need help?"

She still didn't answer.

"I can contact someone for you? Or I have a taxi, I can take you where you need to go, no charge."

"Can you take me back to the hotel, in Sliema?"

"Of course. Come this way."

Jenny followed the man along the high street to a cross road where she saw a line of taxis. The driver opened his cab door and helped her in. Then he got in and started towards Sliema. It was strange leaving the city in the taxi but Jenny was glad that she didn't have to figure out the buses on her own. The taxi driver dropped her outside the hotel.

"Are you sure you will be okay?" he asked.

"Yes, are you sure I can't pay you."

"No, no. Just be safe," he said getting out and opening the door for her.

"Thank you so much," she said heading into the hotel.

She went straight to the lifts and pressed the button to call them repeatedly. One came down. When the doors opened Matthew stepped out.

"What happened?" he asked.

"I'm fine, I'm just going to my room."

Jenny tried to pass him but he stepped back inside the lift with her.

"What happened?" he asked again looking at her torn dress and dirty feet. "Where's Daniel?"

"I'm sorry."

"Why?"

"Is he okay? Are you okay?"

"No," Jenny felt utterly ashamed. "I think I broke his heart."

"Where is he?"

"I left him in the restaurant in Valletta."

"He's still there?"

"I don't know. Please tell him I'm sorry."

They both remained in an uncomfortable silence until the lift came to Jenny's floor where she stepped out. Matthew lingered in the lift but then stopped the doors from closing.

"Should I get Sarah or Lisa?"

"No."

"Can I help?" asked Matthew.

"Take care of Daniel. Please?"

"I will."

Jenny went to her room and closed the door.

## CHAPTER FOURTEEN

Daniel was nervous he wanted to make a future with Jenny but they had avoided the subject. He leaned over the table and kissed her. It felt so risqué kissing her in front of everyone in the restaurant but he did not care. This was the woman he wanted to spend the rest of his life with and he didn't care who knew.

"And you keep doing that," said Jenny, "which makes it so much harder."

Daniel wondered how his kissing her made things harder.

"I love you," said Daniel trying to tell her so much more with so few words.

"And that makes it almost impossible."

"So what do we do?"

Daniel was sure she was playing with him. Teasing him a little but as the waiter returned with their first course he saw how Jenny's expression had changed. What he had at first thought might be playful teasing looked very much more serious and he saw her face change again. Her eyes looked so sad.

"I can't do this to you," said Jenny.

"Do what?"

"Let you love me when I know I'm going to hurt you," she got up and began to leave. "I'm so sorry."

Daniel caught her arm.

"Don't leave."

He began to feel his head spinning. This was not what he was expecting. It was completely removed from any possibility he had imagined for the evening.

"I have to," said Jenny, "please let me go."

"I can't," said Daniel.

He saw the tears in her eyes and he could not hold on to her a moment longer. As soon as he released his hold on her she walked out of the restaurant leaving him so stunned he never thought to follow. Daniel slumped down in his chair. It was only then he realised that several people, including the waiter were looking at him.

"Should I cancel the main course?" the waiter asked uncertainly.

"I don't know," said Daniel.

"I'll give you a minute sir," said the waiter.

Daniel was appreciative of that because at that moment his head was still spinning. What had just happened he kept asking himself? What had he said that pushed her away? He looked at the starter all laid out for two people and then he looked towards where Jenny had left. Was it some kind of joke? He didn't imagine it was and with every second that passed he felt more and more certain that she was not coming back. Jenny was gone. He was by himself and everyone around him knew it.

They had seen what had happened. Daniel began to feel embarrassed. His face became flush and he could feel himself panicking. This was the night they should have been celebrating moving forwards together. Instead the exact opposite had happened. Jenny had broken up with him. Was that really what happened he asked? Surely that is too crazy he thought. They loved each other. They had both said so. She had said so, hadn't she?

"What would you like to do sir?" asked the waiter.

"Can I pay and go, please," said Daniel.

It seemed the waiter had predicted his request and passed him the bill. Daniel looked at it and hurriedly paid so he could leave. He wanted to escape the prying eyes of everyone else in the restaurant as quickly as possible. As soon as he was out of the restaurant he looked around for any sign of Jenny but there was none. He did not even know what he would say if he saw her but then he thought that she was alone in a city and country she didn't really know and he was worried for her. Daniel did the only thing he could and retraced their steps towards the water taxi. There was no sign of her there and so he walked to the bus terminus but she wasn't there either. At that point he did not know where to go or what to do. He loved her but she had taken him by complete surprise. Daniel began to walk, he felt like stumbling into a corner and just hiding there and then he felt something else. His heart began pumping harder and harder and his blood felt toxic as if it was flooding every part of him with anger. He was not sure if he wanted to shout or cry. As he walked he desperately wanted to know and understand what had happened. What about the future had Jenny so scared that she would walk away from him, from his love?

Daniel had walked from the bus station and through Floriana. Out of the city there was a lot less lights. He headed towards the garden he had first taken Jenny to, when they went to Valletta, but the gate was locked by a thick chain and padlock. For a moment Daniel considered turning back. He could catch a bus or go to his grandparent's flat. Neither seemed like the right decision. Instead he followed the coast towards Sliema. When he reached Msida he stopped and looked out into the Mediterranean Sea. To his right were the lights of Valletta and to his left Sliema and beyond his view their hotel. He wanted to be able to rationalise what had happened but he only knew one side of the story. His own. Despite his mind trying to push ideas on him he tried to stay calm. To be rational and logical. The best thing he could do was to find Jenny and to ask her what her side was. Daniel did not want to live with the regret of not knowing. Moreover he still had not given up on the idea of being with Jenny. During their time together he felt as if he had come to know her so well. As if they had known each other completely. Clearly that had not been true. He wondered what he had missed. There was no way for him to know and so he continued walking back towards Sliema. Hoping that the night air could somehow bring him the clarity he was lacking.

The night air did not bring him any insights and after an hour he was outside the hotel. Daniel was not certain if he wanted to go in. He didn't know if Jenny would be there or not. If she was he had no idea what would happen. If she was not there, then he would be equally lost. It was with some trepidation that Daniel entered the hotel. It wasn't Jenny he found but Matthew.

"Are you okay?" asked Matthew.

"Not really."

"What happened?"

"We were at the restaurant. We were just talking and Jenny left. Is she here?"

"Yes."

"I have to see her."

"I don't think that's a good idea."

"Is she okay?"

"Not really. She kept saying she was sorry."

"I'm going to see her."

Matthew stepped in his way.

"Not tonight, okay?"

Daniel did not want to fight with him but he still wanted to see Jenny. He pressed forwards but Matthew held him back.

"Tell me what happened first," said Matthew.

"I don't know."

"What were you talking about before she left."

"I told her I loved her."

"There must be something else."

"We were talking about the future. About what we should do. I don't understand."

"Neither do I but you have to leave it for tonight."

Daniel still did not feel like he was able to but he submitted to Matthew who took him to the elevator and up to their own room.

"Where's Phillip?" asked Daniel.

"He's already asleep. I don't think you're the only one suffering tonight."

"What happened?"

"I don't know. Perhaps we're all different people here," said Matthew.

"Do you know something?"

"Nothing, I swear to you. I would tell you if I knew anything. I saw Jenny come back and she was upset. I tried to help but all she would say is that I should look after you. She didn't want to talk to me or anyone else."

"She was the one."

"There's still time."

"Is there?"

"There is, so for now try and get some rest."

That night the only way Daniel slept was when fatigue overtook his troubled and confused thoughts. Even then he kept waking and every time he woke he wanted to go to Jenny but he remained restrained and waited, wishing the morning would come faster and that the whole night had been nothing but a bad dream.

## CHAPTER FIFTEEN

Daniel did not feel as if he had slept at all and his waking thoughts were the same as those as when he had fallen asleep - all of Jenny. He got up and dressed without disturbing Matthew who was still sleeping. For a moment he paused and listened but he couldn't hear any sound from Phillip's room and so he slipped through the lounge and out into the corridor. He pressed the button for the lift but saw that it was coming up from the ground floor and so took the stairs down to the fifth floor and went over to Jenny's room. With hesitation he knocked on the door. The door pushed open. Daniel went inside, the bedroom door was open but there was no sign of Jenny inside. He looked around in the bedroom. The bed had been slept in but her clothes were gone. For certainty he checked the bathroom. It too was empty. He went back out into the lounge and was about to leave when he saw a note. He picked it up and read it, 'Ibni, ghozz iz-zmien'.

It was the words from the church in Gozo. He put the note in his pocket and continued searching through the hotel literature hoping to find some other clue but there wasn't anything.

As he lingered in the room he could still smell her scent. He tried to remember if he knew what time she was supposed to leave but he did not know. Perhaps she was having breakfast or she was with Sarah and Lisa in their room. They could well have been packing he thought. He had to find her and so Daniel left her room and headed towards Sarah and Lisa's. He knocked on their door. There was no answer so he tried to open it but it was locked. Daniel knocked again and looked around wondering if he had the right room but he was certain he did. He abandoned their room and decided that the next place to check was the restaurant. They could be having breakfast he thought and so he walked to the lift looking back at Sarah and Lisa's room in case the door opened and then at Jenny's room in case she had come back but she hadn't. He still did not want to wait for the lift and so took the stairs to the lobby and then over and down to the restaurant where the first breakfast crowd had gathered. Opening the doors he walked in and began to scan the room for Jenny, Sarah or Lisa. There was no sign of any of them. Daniel returned to the reception and asked the receptionist,

"Have the guests from rooms five-twelve and five-twenty checked out?"

"Let me check."

Daniel waited as the receptionist pressed several buttons on the keyboard.

"Yes sir they are all checked out. Can I help with anything else?"

"No thank you."

She was gone. Daniel did not know what to do and so he sat in the lobby area trying to think. It was not until Matthew came down from the room that he was stirred from his thoughts.

"What's the matter?" asked Matthew.

"She's gone. They all are."

"I didn't think they were leaving till midday."

"Well they're checked out."

"I'm sorry, I thought there would be time."

"I should have gone to her last night."

"She wouldn't have seen you."

"I should have tried."

"You did. I stopped you."

"Why? Why did you stop me?"

"I did what I thought was best."

"I never even got her address or phone number. I've got no way to find her."

"Maybe that's how it is supposed to be?"

"It can't be. It doesn't make any sense."

"No. I guess it doesn't."

"What should I do?" asked Daniel completely lost.

"Let's find her."

"How?"

"They have to be at the airport right?"

"I guess so."

"I'm sure they weren't supposed to leave so early so they'll be there."

"Unless they got an earlier flight."

"Let's go and find out."

Daniel got to his feet.

"A bus or taxi?" asked Matthew.

Daniel shook his head and went over to the

receptionist.

"Can I use the phone please? It's a local call."

"Certainly, press seven for an external line."

He dialled a number and put the headset to his ear and waited. There was a dialling tone and it started to ring.

"Hi, uncle Rocco. Can you help please? Jenny's gone and I need to find her. We think she's at the airport," he listened for a moment. "Thank you."

"Well?" asked Matthew.

"He's on his way."

They moved outside where Daniel paced back and forth as he waited. He did not know what he was going to say to Jenny even if they caught her but he knew he had to at least try and see her one more time. Matthew stayed near him appearing as uncertain of what to say to him as he was to Jenny. Several minutes later Rocco arrived and Daniel wasted no time in jumping in the car. Matthew got in behind him.

"So you've lost Jenny?" asked Rocco.

"Yes. I've got to see her again."

Rocco began driving away.

"The airport yes?"

"We hope so," said Matthew.

"Not to worry we will find her."

There was nothing Daniel could do but worry. He still had not figured out what had caused the breakup. He felt guilty. Imagining there was something he had done or not done that had caused her to leave. Even if they got to the airport on time there was no guarantee that anything he could say would change things. Daniel saw that Rocco was concentrating on driving, his speed increasing.

"We'll make good time," said Rocco.

Despite how quickly they were going Daniel felt as if

the journey was taking too long. He kept imagining that Jenny had already passed through the security checkpoints or that at that very moment she was on board the plane. Even with Rocco taking every short cut he knew and pressing the speed limit it still took them twenty minutes to get to the airport. Rocco pulled up at the departures gate and Daniel hurriedly got out, not waiting for the car to fully stop. He ran inside and looked around. There was a lot of people but at first glance there was no sign of Jenny. Matthew joined him,

"Rocco's got to find somewhere else to park."

"I can't see her."

"Check the departures board."

Daniel and Matthew went over to the display and scanned it for flights to England. There were quite a few and several to different airports in the United Kingdom.

"I don't know which one they'd be on," said Daniel.

"We'll split up. Check each airline's desk," said Matthew.

"Okay. I'm going this way."

Daniel started looking at several different airline's check-in desks, some were closed others had queues of people along with their baggage but he could not see Jenny at any of them or Sarah or Lisa. He began to head back towards where Matthew had gone and saw him talking to Sarah. As he approached he could hear them.

"He only wants a chance to talk to her," said Matthew.

"It's too late," said Sarah.

"At least let him talk to her when we get back."

"I can't."

"Please," said Daniel approaching them both.

"I'm sorry Daniel," said Sarah.

"I just need to know what went wrong."

"It's complicated."

"Can't you simplify it?"

"I can't."

"But I love her."

"It is better this way."

"No. It isn't," said Daniel.

He looked passed Sarah to the security gate and he thought he saw Jenny and Lisa. He ran over to the line.

"Jenny," he shouted, "Jenny."

All the people in the line turned to look at him including Jenny but she turned away as soon as she saw him. Daniel pushed his way through the queue excusing himself as he went and drawing the attention of several security officers. Before he reached her Lisa worked her way towards him and stopped him.

"Let her go," said Lisa.

"I can't. I love her."

"Then you have to let her go, if not for her sake then for your own."

"Why?"

"Because it's what she wants."

"What about what I want?"

Daniel pushed passed her and called out again,

"Jenny."

He saw her try and move forwards but people were not moving as they had become engrossed in what was happening. Daniel forced his way through the last few people and she had no choice but to turn and face him. She looked straight into Daniel's eyes and he swore that she still loved him but she did not move towards him. Two security officers had come over.

"Keep moving," an officer said to the people in line.

The officer started to approach Daniel and Jenny and

he knew he didn't have long.

"Jenny, please tell me what's wrong?"

"Let me go Daniel, please."

"I can't. Not like this, not after everything."

"You have to let me go."

"No."

"It's for your own good. Things should never have gone as far as they did."

"Don't you love me?"

Jenny did not answer, but he knew she did.

"I want to spend my life with you. I want to marry you. To have a family together."

The security officer and everyone near them heard his proposal and all watched and listened. Jenny looked at him but she did not answer and so Daniel dropped to one knee,

"Jenny I love you. You've changed my life and I want to be able to spend every moment of it with you. I know it's soon and that you're afraid of the future but let me be a part of that future. Let me love you. Please."

Daniel couldn't take his eyes from her but he could feel everyone looking at him and every second that ticked by was an eternity. All he wanted, all he needed to hear, was for her to say yes. She looked at him. Her eyes were saying yes, that she loved him but then they began to fill with tears. He hoped they were happy tears, tears of joy.

"I'm so sorry Daniel. I can't."

Jenny turned and tried to get through the queue. The queuers let her through leaving a stunned Daniel behind as she put her bag on the conveyor and went through the metal detector.

"Do you have a boarding pass sir?" asked the security officer.

Daniel stood up and shook his head.

"Please step away from the security area," the officer said.

Daniel knew he had no choice but to comply. He looked back and saw Jenny clearing the metal detector and being quizzed by another officer. She looked back at him and then turned her face from him one last time.

# CHAPTER SIXTEEN

Early that morning Jenny had told Sarah what had happened at the restaurant and that all she wanted to do was to go to the airport and head back. They all checked out of the hotel and took a taxi to the airport where they had waited for the check-in desk to open, so they could go through to the departures lounge. They had waited for several hours but were ready to go through to the lounge when Jenny had seen Matthew and she knew Daniel would not be far away. She asked Sarah to try and delay them both so she could avoid seeing him but the diversion had not worked. Daniel called her name and pressed through the line and was on his knee and pleading with her to let him love her.

She looked at him and she wanted to change her mind to say that they could spend the rest of their lives together but she knew that could not happen. Seeing him again made her feel even worse because she did love him and leaving him was the hardest choice she had ever had to make. Making that same choice twice was almost impossible yet there he was and she knew she had to let him go. She felt her eyes filling with tears and the words almost didn't come out.

"I'm so sorry Daniel. I can't," she said.

Jenny had to leave she couldn't remain there. She did not want to be able to see Daniel any more. To see the pain she had already caused him. The people in the queue let her pass through and so Jenny put her bag on the conveyor belt for the x-ray machine and stepped through the metal detector. At that moment she could not help but look back and she saw Daniel looking at her. It broke her heart completely and she hated herself for what she had done.

"Is everything okay Miss?" asked a female security officer.

"Yes," said Jenny lying.

"Did you know him?"

"Yes."

"Was he bothering you?"

"No."

"Did he ask you to carry anything in your bag or on your person?"

"No."

"Would you stand on the markings. Please lift your arms."

Jenny complied as the officer patted her down.

"Why'd you say no honey?" the officer asked her.

"Because if I said yes then I'd have broken his heart forever."

"I think you already did."

"I'm afraid I did too."

"Well you're clear."

Jenny stepped off the footprint markings and collected her things and then waited for Lisa and Sarah. Lisa was the first to join her.

"Are you okay?" asked Lisa.

"No," said Jenny.

"You did the right thing."

"Are you sure?"

"Yes."

"I should have told him."

"What difference would it have made?"

"At least he would have known the truth. He might not have hated me."

"He'll get over it."

"I'm not sure he will."

"It's what men do. They don't feel things like we do."

"Daniel was different."

"They're all the same."

"No. They're not and I think I've made a terrible mistake."

Jenny moved towards the security check point but Lisa stopped her.

"You have to let him go."

"I don't want to."

"You've done the right thing. You said so yourself. This is better for him in the long run."

"I don't care. I love him."

Jenny looked at the security area for a way to get back out but she couldn't see any obvious path. It was like a one way valve.

"Daniel."

Her voice was soft and broken.

"It's too late. He's already gone," said Lisa trying to

convince her to stay.

"No," sobbed Jenny.

It took a while for Sarah to join them and she did all she could to try and comfort Jenny. During the wait to board the plane and the flight back Jenny could feel herself fading away. By the time they landed her skin was paler than before they had left and she felt as if she were little more than a hollow shell filled with pain.

## CHAPTER SEVENTEEN

Matthew and Rocco both understood everything they needed to know as they took Daniel back from the airport to the hotel. Rocco parked the car near the hotel and helped get Daniel back to his room where he cracked open the mini bar.

"This isn't going to help," said Rocco holding up the miniature bottles. "I'll go and get a proper sized bottle. Look after him Matthew, hey?"

"I will."

Rocco left Matthew and Daniel in their lounge. They heard a door open and Phillip emerged from his slumber.

"What's going on? What's with all the noise?" asked Phillip.

Daniel didn't say anything. He felt terrible.

"You look awful," said Phillip.

"Phillip," rebuked Matthew.

"Well he does. What happened?"

"Jenny's gone."

"Okay, and?"

"They broke up."

"Oh," said Phillip thinking about it. "I didn't know you were together."

Even in his heart broken state Daniel felt astounded by his brother.

"Where have you been?" asked Matthew.

"Right here. With you guys."

"Are you sure?"

"Yes of course."

"So you didn't notice all the days and nights he wasn't here?" said Matthew.

"Yes he was."

"No I wasn't," said Daniel finding a little of his voice.

"You were too. I would have noticed if you weren't."

"Clearly not," said Matthew.

Rocco returned with a large bottle of whiskey.

"I bought it from the bar," said Rocco.

"Uncle Rocco," said Phillip, "what are you doing here?"

"I took your brother to the airport."

"What? When? Why?"

"By gods you're as blind as your father," said Rocco.

"Would someone tell me what the hell is going on?"

"Sit down," said Rocco.

He took all the glasses and cups from the bar and poured an unhealthy measure of whiskey in each before handing them out.

"Drink," said Rocco to Daniel, "and start at the beginning."

Gradually Daniel, assisted by Matthew and Rocco, retold his story. By the end Phillip was stunned and forced to admit that even when they had been right in front of him he had been blind. Phillip did not try platitudes or clichéd words of advice. He didn't have any. That in itself seemed like a first to Daniel. In the retelling of the story of his falling in love with Jenny he also began to realise that he too had perhaps been blind. There was something he had missed and that thought continued to eat away at the back of his mind. With the story over Daniel wanted to sleep. He didn't want to feel any more and so he said to his friends and family that he was going to lie down and he went into the bedroom and slept until the evening.

When he woke he went to freshen up in the bathroom and then went back out into the lounge. He was surprised to see his grandfather on the settee reading a newspaper.

"Daniel, my boy. Come here."

His grandfather stood up and hugged him.

"She is gone but you are not, you must remember that."

Daniel tried not to cry. He did not want to cry in front of his grandfather.

"I loved her so much."

"She loved you too."

"Why did she leave me?"

"Sometimes there is no choice."

"I gave her a choice. I asked her to stay."

"You offered her a choice but she may not have had one. Do you understand?"

"No."

"My poor boy."

William gave Daniel his handkerchief.

"Sometimes we only see things from our own perspective," said William. "To you she had a choice but for her there was none."

"So what do I do?" asked Daniel.

"Show her the other choice."

"I tried."

"You must try again."

"I can't."

"Why not?"

"She doesn't want me to."

"I think she does. Find a way to show her she can choose you."

"How? I don't even know how to find her."

"That part is simple. Rocco will get her address?"

"How?"

"The hotel has it."

Daniel felt immensely grateful for his friends and family. Even in his worst moments they were supporting him, doing everything they possibly could to ensure his happiness. It was more than he could ever have hoped for.

"Now we must eat," said William as he opened the door, "come let's eat."

Daniel followed his grandfather from his room and down to the restaurant where Matthew, Phillip, Charlotte, Rocco and Violet were all waiting for him. Both Charlotte and his grandmother showered him with hugs and kisses. They all had a late meal together and slowly but surely Daniel began to feel stronger again.

The next day was their last day in Malta before they would fly back in the early hours of the morning. Daniel still was not quite at full strength but last night had shown him how important his family was to him and so they visited his grandparents one more time. Daniel was trying not to talk about Jenny but she was always on his mind. Before they left his grandparent's apartment he recalled the note Jenny had left behind from the church in Gozo and he asked William what it meant,

"Cherish time my son," William told him.

The words stayed with him. He would cherish the time they had all spent together and the moments he and Jenny had shared. Even if they were the only moments they had he would hold onto them forever.

The day passed faster than Daniel expected with visiting family, packing, checking passports and times and late that night Rocco came to take them all to the airport. There was no hurry this time. Rocco somehow managed to squeeze all their bags into the boot of his car and they made their way to the airport. They looked out over the bay at Valletta, illuminated against the night sky and Daniel knew he would miss the place and his family but he had a sense of hope that he would return and it would not be alone. He watched the road much of the way to the airport feeling that it was all a journey, one long trip to get to a certain destination. In that moment his mind was clear and he knew that his end point was to be with Jenny once more. Rocco parked at the airport and went with them into the terminal. He saw them through the check-in and to the security gate. There he handed Jenny's address to Daniel and wished them all good luck and a safe flight. They shook hands and parted ways.

All Daniel could think about was Jenny the whole journey back. He wished she was sitting next to him. In his mind he could see Jenny's face and he relived the happy times they had had together. Every detail seemed clearer than the actual moment. Daniel could not wait to be off the plane and hoped that he would soon be able to hold Jenny in his arms again. He wanted to feel her body pressing against his as he kissed her and she let him love her. The plane flew over the Mediterranean Sea, through the night clouds of hopes and dreams and over Europe until it crossed the Channel and in the early hours of the morning they looked out over the coast of England. They all knew they were home but Daniel felt that this was a new start. A chance to build a home with Jenny. He envisaged them sitting together watching the sunrise. The plane continued its descent and began slowing down. Daniel felt the kick of force. He looked out and saw London beneath them. Somewhere down there, he knew, Jenny was. He checked his pocket for her address and was reassured to feel the paper still in its place. The aeroplane began turning and lining up for its final descent. The cabin became filled with the noise of the engines as they rapidly lost altitude and after a few minutes they all felt the solid thud of the back wheels touching down. A moment later the front came down and they were on the ground. The plane continued to rapidly slow down and with its speed shed the noise diminished. From that point it was a matter of waiting. Waiting for the plane to stop taxiing, for the tunnel to be connected, for the doors to be opened, for people to open the luggage compartments, negotiate their bags in the tight space and then start to leave. Daniel, Matthew and Phillip all shuffled along through the plane to the front exit and then walked through the tunnel and into the terminal. They used the moving walkways to speed them along as fast as they could go until they were stopped by passport control.

There always seemed to be a queue no matter how fast you disembarked or how many people you passed along the way. They waited their turn and gradually people trickled to the other side where they could wait once more for their baggage. The three of them passed through passport control relatively quickly and waited at baggage claim for the conveyor belt to spring to life. It did. Delivering only one bag at first. Then it stopped. It came back to life and delivered a few more. None of them were their cases. After a while the conveyor moved again and continued to deliver bags. They worked together to pull their bags and load them onto a trolley as quickly as they could and then went through customs. They cleared customs and emerged in the arrivals lounge.

"What's your plan?" asked Matthew.

"I'm going to find Jenny."

"Why don't we drop our bags off at my flat then we'll come with you."

"You don't have to," said Daniel.

"We've come this far together we're not going to leave you now."

"No we're not," said Phillip.

"Lead the way then," said Daniel.

Matthew led them to the underground where the train was waiting. It soon filled up with returning holiday makers and they were on their way.

"Where does she live?" asked Matthew.

Daniel took the paper from his pocket and handed it to Matthew.

"We'll have to cross the river and we'll need a map."

"Okay."

Daniel and Phillip followed Matthew from the underground to his flat where they dropped their bags and Matthew grabbed his London street map before they turned round to leave. They took a bus across the river and Matthew made his best guess as to where they should get off and then they were on foot. Compared to where they had been London seemed like another world. They were surrounded by small, grimy looking shops in near derelict buildings. The decay was everywhere. It even seemed to affect the sky as it was grey with dark threatening clouds. It did not deter any of them and Daniel continued putting his faith in Matthew who led them along several streets. The area became more residential with rows upon rows of terraced houses, most with bay windows and three stories high.

"I think this is it," said Matthew pointing to one house.

Daniel looked at the paper. The street name, the house number all matched. All he had to do was ring the doorbell.

"We'll wait right here," said Matthew.

"Go on," said Phillip.

Daniel walked up to the front door. He did not want to get rejected for a third time but he also knew he was not able to live with how they had left things and so he rang the bell. There was no answer. Daniel took a step back and looked at the house. He could not tell if there was anyone inside.

"Ring it again," said Phillip.

Daniel rang it again and waited but there was still no answer. Phillip came over and pushed and held the ringer.

"There's no one here," said Daniel.

Phillip stopped ringing the bell. Daniel turned to leave but Phillip started banging loudly on the door.

"Phillip, it's no use. There's no one here."

"I'm not going to let you give up that easily," said Phillip.

"Maybe we can come back later?" said Matthew.

"I don't know if there's any point," said Daniel feeling like giving up.

Phillip resumed banging on the door and ringing the doorbell but even to him it was becoming clear that no one was home.

"I guess there's no point calling," said Matthew.

"Not really," said Daniel.

"So now what?" asked Phillip.

"I don't know."

"There was a café a few streets over. We could get something to eat then come back," said Matthew.

"Sounds good to me," said Phillip; only thinking with his stomach.

Daniel looked back at the house and knew there was little else they could do. They walked back to the café. Matthew and Phillip both ordered a full English breakfast whilst Daniel's nerves had taken the edge off his appetite and so he settled on a bacon sandwich. They sat down to eat at a table.

"It's good to be home," said Phillip without thinking.

"It was a good break even though, well you know," said Matthew.

"It was good," said Daniel.

"We're not done yet," said Phillip.

Daniel didn't want to be done but a part of him thought that perhaps he should be. Jenny had already pushed him away twice and he didn't see why it would be any different the third time. He kept thinking about all the reasons why she might have done it but he could not fathom one that seemed to make any sense to him. Daniel finished his sandwich long before Matthew and Phillip and he didn't want to wait.

"I'm going back," said Daniel.

"Wait," said Matthew still eating.

"I'll wait on her door step but I can't wait here."

"We'll come with you," said Phillip.

"Finish eating."

"Do you know the way?" asked Matthew.

"Yes," said Daniel getting up and leaving.

Daniel walked back to Jenny's house. Nothing seemed to have changed but he still went up and rang the doorbell. Once more there was no answer. Daniel knocked. Again no reply. He turned around and sat on the doorstep. There wasn't a lot of activity. The occasional car, the odd person now and again. Each time a new person or car came by he wondered if it might be Jenny but none of them were. If she wasn't at home where was she? He wondered if she had gone with Sarah and Lisa. What if the first people he met were her parents? What would they be like? What would they make of him? What would he say to them? Once again he felt as if he had nothing but questions when all he wanted was answers. An elderly lady was walking along the street and looked at him suspiciously.

"Hello," said Daniel.

"Good morning."

She kept on walking. Daniel stood up and looked around. He thought about going back to the café and telling Phillip and Matthew it was over. Wasn't that his choice? Couldn't he choose for it to be over? His mind was made up, he would keep the good memories he had with Jenny and try to move on. It felt as if that was what she wanted him to do. Why then wasn't he moving he asked himself? Why stay? Why even try to find her? The only reason he kept coming back to was because he loved her and he could not stop loving her. He saw Matthew and Phillip hurriedly walking towards him.

"I'm sorry," said Phillip.

"Why?"

"I called Lisa."

"Okay."

"She said that Jenny's in hospital."

"What? No. I don't understand," said Daniel. "Was there an accident?"

"No," said Matthew. "She's sick but that's about all we know."

"She'll be okay right?" asked Daniel.

"We don't know," said Matthew.

Daniel looked at his brother but something in his expression told him that he had grave doubts.

"I've got to see her."

"I'll get you there."

Matthew was true to his word. He took them back across the river and through street after street of terraced houses and then past rows of shops until they arrived at the hospital. All Daniel could think of was how vibrant she had been the whole time they were together but now he felt he was closer to understanding why she had made the choice she had.

# Chapter Eighteen

Daniel entered Jenny's hospital room and saw Sarah. Sarah saw him and then so did Jenny. She was hooked up to machines and monitoring devices. Her skin had lost its glow and was unnaturally white. Sarah stood up and came over to him,

"You shouldn't be here."

"No, it's okay," said Jenny, her voice weak.

Sarah stepped aside and let Daniel pass. He went to Jenny and wanted to kiss her but with all the tubes and wires it was impossible to do anything other than kiss her forehead.

"Hi," said Daniel.

"Hi."

"You are still beautiful."

Jenny tried to smile but it was exhausting. Daniel saw the effort it took her and wished he could hold her again or do anything to make her feel better.

"So this is the complication?" asked Daniel.

"Yes."

"You're sick."

"I'm dying."

"No. You can't be."

"It's too late Daniel. Only a matter of when now."

"But I love you."

"And I loved you but you have to let me go."

"I won't. Not whilst we can have a single moment together."

"I didn't want this," said Jenny.

"No one would."

"Not the cancer. I didn't want to hurt you like this."

Daniel wanted to know if there was some chance, any chance but he couldn't ask.

"It's leukaemia and because I'm special it's incurable," said Jenny.

"You are special."

"And incurable."

Jenny tried to smile again but the effort was too much and her lips were dry. Daniel took a little water and wiped them. She kissed his finger.

"You gave me a gift," said Jenny, "one I never thought I'd experience. You showed me things I had never imagined and made me feel so alive."

"I wanted to do more. For us to have more time."

"If I did then I would have chosen you. I would have married you."

"And we would have been happy."

"We were happy."

Daniel could see that Jenny was getting tired but he did not want to leave her.

"Let her rest," said Sarah.

"I'm going to be right here," Daniel told Jenny.

She was already sleeping.

Sarah tenderly took Daniel's arm and walked with him out of Jenny's room and quietly closed the door.

"I'm sorry," said Sarah to Daniel, Matthew and Phillip.

"She could have told me," said Daniel.

"She wanted to but it got more difficult the longer you were together."

"And now?"

"Now all we can do is wait."

"Is there really nothing we can do?"

"I'm afraid not. Her parents explored every option."

"Where are they?" asked Daniel.

"They're here. I was sitting with Jenny whilst they went to the cafeteria. They haven't had a break since we got back."

"What happened?" asked Matthew.

"Nothing," said Sarah.

"But she seemed okay."

"She hid it well and we helped her. We helped her do what she wanted. To have one last adventure," said Sarah to Daniel, "and you loved her and made her so happy and I will always be grateful to you for that."

Daniel felt that his world was falling apart. Everything had come together. He at last understood why Jenny had pushed him away but now it was all crumbling away again. There was nothing he could do. He felt useless. The next few hours went by incredibly slowly and in that time Daniel met Jenny's parents. Despite the circumstances of their meeting they were glad to find people that cared about their daughter so much and when Jenny woke they were happy to hear her recount some of the wonders Daniel had shown her. She told them about the Blue

Grotto, the cathedrals, Popeye's Village and about how incredibly friendly Daniel's family had been to her.

At times Daniel watched Jenny and she struggled to breath, her body was so young but now completely crippled by illness. As Jenny continued to worsen she had to have an oxygen mask which made it harder for her to speak but she still tried to smile whenever she saw Daniel. All he could do was hold her hand and never give up. Her parents let him stay with her hour after hour. They kept a vigil with her for three days and nights after which a doctor brought the prognosis that Jenny was near the end now. Daniel turned to look at Jenny, her beautiful features so cold. Still Jenny struggled but he could not hear what she was saying. Daniel took off her oxygen mask and Jenny reached up towards him. He bent down and she wrapped her arms around his neck.

"Not here please," said Jenny.

He was not certain what he should do but Jenny's mother began unhooking her from the machines.

"I want to be with you," said Jenny.

Daniel picked her up in his arms, she was so light he was afraid she was already gone. Her hair pressed on his arm as he supported her head and her legs felt cold against his other arm. Jenny's father cleared the way ahead of Daniel. Sarah picked up a blanket. The doctor bowed his head and then raised it again to say he was sorry but they all knew he had done all that he could which was all anyone could have done. Daniel carried Jenny through the hospital and up to the roof. No one said anything or tried to stop them. They only watched in solemn silence. Jenny's father forced open the door and Daniel stepped out onto the flat roof with Jenny in his arms. The roof had a small wall around it made up by the edges of the building and there were several potted plants and flowers in one corner. Daniel walked over to the corner overlooking the city. His arms were buckling but he never let Jenny go. Daniel knelt down and propped Jenny up against him so she could look out over the city. Sarah covered her with the blanket. The sky was still overcast but in the distance they could see St. Paul's Cathedral. The sun broke through the clouds and made the skyline appear silhouetted.

"Are we back?" asked Jenny.

Daniel looked at the city and saw how much the outline looked like Valletta.

"We will always be there," said Daniel.

Jenny struggled to turn towards Daniel. He helped move her so she could see him and everyone she loved. Looking into her eyes Daniel saw that her love was endless. Jenny tried to tilt her head so she could kiss Daniel. Softly he kissed her. His whole world merged with her and he felt his heart beating wildly. Jenny gasped as he pulled away but he continued to hold her in his arms. He was transfixed by her eyes, her heart and her soul but as the clouds blocked the sun he felt how cold she was becoming. Jenny's life drained away and her whole body became limp. Still Daniel held her. He rocked back and forth and cried out,

"No!"

The clouds parted and the sun struck Jenny. For a minute her whole body glowed a soft golden colour and her eyes shone with the sun. The light danced over her body like a hundred angels and filled her body with warmth. Daniel wished that she would come back to him but then the clouds blocked the sun once more and all he could see was Jenny's pale lifeless form. Jenny's mother knelt by his side and with shaking hands softly closed Jenny's eye lids.

"Sleep my baby girl."

Daniel hoped Jenny would sleep in peace but his mind and body were filled with pain. His tears streaked down his cheeks and fell onto Jenny and it seemed as if she too was crying.

Made in the USA
Middletown, DE
25 July 2015